OHIO TRAIL MIX
Adventures and Inspiration Along the Ohio Literary Trail

By
Bettie Boswell
JPC Allen
Rebecca Waters
Betty Kulich
Michelle L. Levigne

www.YeOldeDragonBooks.com

Ye Olde Dragon Books
P.O. Box 30802
Middleburg Hts., OH 44130

www.YeOldeDragonBooks.com

2OldeDragons@gmail.com

ISBN 13: 978-1-952345-88-3

Published in the United States of America
Publication Date: December 1, 2022

Cover Art © Copyright Ye Olde Dragon Books 2022

TABLE OF CONTENTS

THE OHIO LITERARY TRAIL
Presented by Ohioana Library Association
http://www.ohioana.org/

Interested in the map of the Ohio Literary Trail, and more information?
http://www.ohioana.org/resources/the-ohio-literary-trail-2/

The Ohio Literary Trail, presented by the Ohioana Library Association, shines a spotlight on Ohio's role in shaping culture and literature worldwide. Visitors will discover the state's rich literary landscape through landmark destinations, historical markers that recognize literary achievements, and book festivals dedicated to readers and writers. Organized by the state's five geographic regions for a convenient self-guided driving tour, The Ohio Literary Trail encourages exploration by tourists planning a literary-themed outing, as well as Ohioans who want to discover literary treasures they never knew existed in their own backyard.

NORTHWEST OHIO
Literary Destinations
1. **Clyde Historical Museum** with Sherwood Anderson marker (Clyde, Sandusky County)
2. **Toledo-Lucas County Public Library- Nancy Drew Exhibit** with Toledo's First High School and Toledo Lucas County Public Library marker (Toledo, Lucas County)
3. **The Mazza Museum** (Findlay, Hancock County)
Literary Markers
4. The Brumback Library (Van Wert, Van Wert County)
5. House of Four Pillars (Maumee, Lucas County)
6. Lois Lenski (Anna, Shelby County)
7. Paulding County Carnegie Library (Paulding, Paulding County)
8. Sandusky Library (Sandusky, Erie County)

Book Festival: Claire's Day (Maumee, Lucas County)

NORTHEAST OHIO

Literary Destinations

9. <u>Haines House </u>(Alliance, Stark County)

10. <u>Malabar Farm</u> with <u>Louis Bromfield</u> marker (Lucas, Richland County)

11. <u>Oak Hill Cottage</u> (Mansfield, Richland County)

12. <u>Ohio Center for the Book at Cleveland Public Library</u> (Cleveland, Cuyahoga County)

13. <u>Wick Poetry Center</u> and <u>Reinberger Children's Library Center</u> (Kent, Portage County)

Literary Markers

14. <u>Daniel Carter Beard</u> (Painesville, Lake County)

15. <u>Bristol Public Library</u> (Bristolville, Trumbull County)

16. <u>Cleveland Heights-University Heights Public Library – Harvey Pekar</u> (Cleveland Heights, Cuyahoga County)

17. <u>Hart Crane</u> (Garrettsville/Portage County)

18. <u>East Cleveland Public Library</u> (East Cleveland, Cuyahoga County)

19. <u>James Mercer Langston Hughes</u> (Cleveland, Cuyahoga County)

20. <u>The Oxcart Library</u> (North Olmsted, Cuyahoga County)

21. <u>Earl Derr Biggers</u> (Warren, Trumbull County)

22. <u>Helen Steiner Rice</u> and Toni Morrison (Lorain, Lorain County)

23. <u>The Second High School – Burton Public Library</u> (Burton, Geauga County)

24. <u>Home of Superman</u> (Cleveland, Cuyahoga County)

Book Festival: <u>Buckeye Book Fair</u> (Wooster, Wayne County)

CENTRAL OHIO

Literary Destinations

25. <u>Thurber House Museum and Thurber Center</u> with <u>James Thurber</u> marker (Columbus, Franklin County)

26. <u>The Billy Ireland Cartoon Library & Museum</u> and <u>Jerome Lawrence and Robert E. Lee Theatre Research Institute</u>(Columbus, Franklin County)

27. <u>Ohioana Library Association</u> (Columbus, Franklin County)

28. <u>Wagnalls Memorial Library</u> (Lithopolis, Fairfield County)

Billy Ireland Cartoon Museum (Jodi Miller photo)

Literary Markers

29. <u>Columbus Metropolitan Main Library</u> (Columbus, Franklin County)

30. <u>Dawn Powell</u> (Mt. Gilead/Morrow County)

31. John Crowe Ransom and The Kenyon Review (Gambier, Knox County)
32. Wilbur H. Siebert Collection (Columbus, Franklin County)

Book Festival: **Ohioana Book Festival** (Columbus, Franklin County)

SOUTHWEST OHIO
Literary Destinations
33. **Harriet Beecher Stowe House** with Harriet Beecher Stowe marker (Cincinnati, Hamilton County)
34. **Paul Laurence Dunbar House and State Memorial** with Paul Laurence Dunbar marker (Dayton, Montgomery County)
35. **McGuffey Museum** with William Holmes McGuffey House (Oxford, Butler County)
36. **The Mercantile Library** (Cincinnati, Hamilton County)
37. **The Rankin House** (Ripley, Brown County)
Literary Markers
38. Natalie Clifford Barney (Dayton, Montgomery County)
39. Hallie Quinn Brown (Wilberforce, Greene County)
40. Milton Caniff (Hillsboro, Highland County)
41. Virginia Hamilton (Yellow Springs, Greene County)
42. William Dean Howells (Hamilton, Butler County)
43. Fannie Hurst (Hamilton, Butler County)
44. McCloskey Museum (Hamilton, Butler County)
45. Percy MacKaye-"The Poet's Shack" (Oxford, Butler County)
46. The Jacob Rader Marcus Center of the American Jewish Archives (Cincinnati, Hamilton County)
47. Albert Nelson Marquis/Who's Who (Decatur, Brown County)
48. Public Library of Cincinnati and Hamilton County (Cincinnati, Hamilton County)
49. Helen Hooven Santmyer (Xenia, Greene County)
50. Wilmington Library (Wilmington, Clinton County)

Book Festival: **Books by the Banks** (Cincinnati, Hamilton County)

SOUTHEAST OHIO
Literary Destinations
51. **Dard Hunter marker** (Chillicothe, Ross County)
52. **National Road and Zane Grey Museum** with Zane Grey marker (Norwich, Muskingum County)
53. **Grandma Gatewood Trail** *(South Bloomingville, Hocking County)*
Literary Markers

54. <u>James Edwin Campbell</u> and Ambrose Meigs (Pomeroy, Meigs County)
55. <u>Frances Dana Gage</u> (McConnelsville, Morgan County)
56. <u>William Dean Howells</u> (Martins Ferry, Belmont County)
57. <u>Putnam Family Library – Belpre Farmers Library</u> (Belpre, Washington County)
58. <u>Burton Egbert Stevenson</u> (Chillicothe, Ross County)
59. <u>Tessa Sweazy Webb</u> (Logan, Hocking County)
60. <u>Western Library Association – The Coonskin Library</u> (Amesville, Athens County)
61. <u>James Arlington Wright</u> (Martins Ferry, Belmont County)

Book Festival: <u>Spring Literary Festival</u> (Athens, Athens County)

During 2022, members of ACFW-Ohio gave themselves a challenge: to visit as many of the Ohio Literary Trail locations near them as possible. And, if inspired by the literary people and places and events, write a story. Covid, distance, weather and life in general got in the way of many of us getting together, but we persisted and we dreamed, and we present to you the stories.

Will there be more stories inspired and written in 2023?

Time will tell!

We hope you enjoy our flights of imagination.

MAZZA MYSTERY
By Bettie Boswell

The eerie quiet sent a chill down my back. It had been a while since I entered the darkened doorway of the Mazza Museum. Normally children's voices spilled from the galleries, but not on this thundery afternoon in late July. During the school year docent duties kept me busy working with touring students. Today the place was as silent as a shadowed tomb. The strange trickle of foreboding that ran down my spine didn't make sense in this normally happy place.

I'd made arrangements to conduct a private tour for two of my friends, on one of the days the collection of children's book illustrations didn't open to the public. My pals had time on their hands. The Mazza Museum needed more recruits--people who were not afraid to face a band of chattering children. As a retired teacher, the connection with kids came easy for me. I hoped it would be the same for my duo of buddies. I had no doubt about Marla fitting in, since she'd been a librarian and Sunday school teacher. Peggy, a retired 911 operator turned quilter, might be another matter due to her quiet nature. Perhaps her skills as a grandmother would help. Nerves of steel as an emergency medical operator under pressure might pay off, too.

"Hey Jo Ann, we're here."

I almost jumped out of my skin as Marla's melodic voice echoed across the atrium at the same time thunder rumbled overhead. Peggy followed close behind, with a wave from across the room as she studied the replica of a dinosaur skeleton suspended from the ceiling.

"Hi ladies, I'm so glad you could come. I really like volunteering here and hope you will think about joining me."

We shared welcoming hugs and then headed into the darkened museum. Movement-sensitive lights began to flicker on as we entered. The lighting in the first room seemed to have trouble stabilizing. The strobe light effect bounced across the display of white plaster hands, cast from illustrator's artistic fingers. The effect was disturbing and not the first impression I'd hoped for my friends.

"I'm sorry. There must be a short in the wires due to the storm," I apologized as the light reflected off Marge's thick glasses.

"The effect goes along with the dinosaur in the other room. It's kind of exciting in a weird way." Peggy leaned closer to one of the plaster forms. "Is there blood on this hand? It looks like there's a brown spot on one of the fingers. I wonder if that person needed to call 911 after this plaster experiment went bad."

She still had her morbid sense of humor when it came to accidents and death. The boy visitors might find her entertaining if she added her own take to the tours. I wasn't so sure about squeamish girls. Squeamish kind of described the feeling in my gut at the moment. The flashing lights were starting to give me a headache.

Marla's voice cooed from the other side of the room. "Look at this hand. I always enjoyed reading Rosemary Wells' *Max* books at story time. The little ones liked Max because of the cartoons. At least those stories held their attention. Oh look, there's Marc Brown and Arthur." Her high-pitched voice wasn't helping my developing headache. I should be showing my friends around the museum. Instead, I just wanted those lights to settle down to a solid stream and stop putting on a bizarre show. Like an answer to prayer, the commotion ended and I started to focus on the objects around me.

At that moment my eyes fell on the latest addition to the display. There were illustrator's hands I'd never seen before. At first, I didn't recognize any of the new artists' names. Then I spotted a whimsical painting above a well-shaped woman's hand. The signature on the bottom of the artwork revealed a familiar pair of capital B's sitting back-to-back and made to look like the wings of a bee. I did a double and a triple take before I checked out the placard. Sure enough, the name was that of an old friend from my growing up days, Bea Bidwell.

I hadn't seen her in years. We lost contact after graduating from high school. She'd been good at art back then. It looked like her works were now those of a professional illustrator. However, there was one big problem: the perfect plaster hand. There was no way that it was my Bea's.

"There's an imposter in the house. Someone has stolen the identity of my childhood friend. I am going to find out who did this and bring them out of their evil shadows." I planted my fists on my hips, ready to fight for the right.

"Should we call the police? I'm sure they'd be able to help." Peggy lifted her flip phone, ready to call whenever I gave her the go ahead.

I wasn't quite ready to take action, yet. My head still pounded and I needed to be able to think straight. I held up a hand and shook my head. I thought I'd fall over from the stars that started circling.

Marla tucked a finger under her double chin and looked thoughtful. "I'm pretty good at solving mysteries. Curating the Nancy Drew display in the children's library in Toledo made me a great sleuth. We need to start collecting evidence that will help the police. If they can't solve the mystery, then we will. Uh, what exactly are we investigating?"

"Yeah, this looks like a pretty nice painting and set of fingers to me." Peggy laid a comforting hand on my arm and gave it a squeeze. She had a gift for knowing when a person felt bad.

"That's the problem. Those fingers are too perfect. Bea's mother may have taken the drug, thalidomide, when she was pregnant with my friend. Bea only had short stubs for two of her fingers. We used sign language where I taught school and the sign for *I love you* kind of resembled the birth defect to her useable hand. Her other arm and hand didn't work too well." I held up my palm and bent down the middle and ring finger to form the sign, which was a combination of the letters L and I.

I spoke in a softer voice so no one beside my friends could hear. "Bea did wonders with art materials. She used what she had and created pieces that won first place at school art shows. She even had a couple pieces that went to the state fair during high school."

Marla whipped out a small notepad from her purse. "How can you be sure this art is done by the same person?" She grabbed a pen and had it poised over the paper. "The name may only be a coincidence."

I was ready to hand over the first clue as I pointed to the illustration. "Look at the signature on the original artwork. Bea signed all her art with that exact design. If you look close at the insect's wings you can see her name spelled out in the veins."

Two gray heads leaned in close to check my observation. Peggy pulled a pair of purple readers from the depths of her quilted bag. "I see what you mean. Maybe she had some kind of surgery to fix her hand. I took a call once where a man accidentally chopped off one of his fingers. It was quite a miracle. A surgery specialist was at the hospital at the right time. A good sewing job took care of that fellow's problem."

"Do you see any scars on the hand that is supposed to be hers? I sure can't." I pointed to the perfect palm.

"Not that I can see. How about you, Marla, do you spot any stitches?" Peggy looked perplexed as she stepped away.

Marla looked down her nose, through the lower part of her bifocals, and shook her head. "The digits look perfectly connected. There isn't a clue here."

I searched below the display to find the information notebook that sat on the bottom shelf. As I flipped through the pages, they contained plenty of data about books completed but very little about the illustrator's personal life. When I searched for a picture of her face, the booklet only contained words.

I blew a breath out that ruffled my freshly trimmed bangs. My outing to convince my friends to volunteer as Mazza docents had turned into a big mystery. Then a thought crossed my mind. The exhibit only included hands of artists who had come to the museum. Most of them had spoken at the annual conference earlier in the month. I'd missed it this year due to traveling to see a newborn grandchild. Maybe the office had photographs or even a video of the woman who now answered to the name Bea Bidwell.

"You two check out the rest of this gallery for a few minutes. I'm going to see if someone is in the office. Maybe they will have a picture or video of the woman."

"We'll be waiting right here." Peggy made her way over to a painting featuring a quilt as part of the subject matter.

Marla moved closer to one featuring a book cover. "Oh, look, I read this one at least once a year to the children who came to the library for the summer reading program."

I headed out the museum door and made a sharp right into the office. The big wigs were out for the rest of the week, but the secretary promised to ask them about pictures and videos. The bosses had sent the videos to an outside firm for editing and the finished films wouldn't be ready for another month. I tried to contain my frustration, but she must have sensed it growing.

"Try to not worry, ma'am. I'll let them know you are anxious to see the videos. You can expect a call as soon as we get them."

I nodded and left the room before I said something I shouldn't. The woman was trying to be courteous, but it irked me when she called me *ma'am*. I wasn't that old yet, was I? At the moment, I wasn't sure. It felt like I had the weight of the museum's *Cat in the Hat* statue dragging from my shoulders as I trudged back to the museum.

I heard giggles coming from one of the side rooms. My pals had discovered the pop-up book collection. I found them playing with the tabs, making superheroes burst off the page. I forced my face to form a pleasant smile and began giving them the best docent tour I could pull off. We moved through the rest of the galleries, exploring the amazing world of children's illustration. I hoped I did a convincing job presenting the displays, but my mind kept returning to the mysterious hand that did not belong to my childhood friend.

~~~~~

The next day, I dug an old box out of Mom's attic. She was in a retirement home these days, but I hadn't had the heart to start going through the house. Today seemed like a good time to start, especially if I could uncover something about Bea. Back in the days before email and texting, we had kept up a pretty good conversation through passing notes in class. I had boxed up a few of them along with some actual letters we'd mailed to each other when we headed off to college. I lived with Mom to save money while going to teacher's college. Bea had headed off on an art scholarship to some out-of-state college. Gradually the letters had faded along with our close friendship. The last I heard, she had moved in with a cousin in Cleveland and did art for a greeting card company.

I had started sorting through the papers when I heard a knock at the door. Marla and Peggy promised to help me before we parted ways the day before. We all sat around the table looking for pages with Bea's name.
~~~~~

"Look, here's one with that double B bee. It does look exactly like the signature in the museum's gallery." Marla held up a pencil sketched caricature of one of my junior high teachers.

I chuckled. "It was a wonder that we survived math class that year. We made a game out of passing notes and confusing Mr. Hitchcock with our nonsense questions."

Peggy reached deep into the box and dug out a handful of black-and-white photographs. After a few moments of looking at them through her purple readers, she held one up for us all to see. "Is this Bea? It looks like she's holding a prize in her hand."

Marla and I bent over her shoulder to take a closer look. "Yes, this is what my friend looked like in school."

"This picture definitely shows her affected hand. Once we get a picture of the imposter, we can compare this one with it." Marla whipped out her notebook and wrote down the latest clues.

We sorted through the rest of the box and found a letter with a Cleveland address. The missive inside indicated Bea lived with her cousin at that address. It was one of the last letters I'd gotten from her before we quit writing.

"You should write a letter to that address and see if anyone answers, or if they provide a forwarding address. I wonder if we could find a phone number for that house. My grandchildren could use the internet to see if one is available." Peggy pulled out her phone and made a quick call to her daughter. She turned to the rest of us. "Sorry, the grandchildren are away at church camp for the week. No phones allowed."

Once she shared the information with the rest of us, I decided to write a note. After picking up a pen, I stopped. "How about going on an adventure, ladies? I've always wanted to see The Rock and Roll Hall of Fame. We can just happen to be in the neighborhood and use it as an excuse to check out this address."

"Cool! Are you driving?" Marla seemed relieved when I nodded. She didn't enjoy driving to faraway places.

"I'd be glad to drive. I've gone over there several times to see one of my fellow retired teachers, so I know the route pretty well."

"Good. I'd hate to have to call my buddies at 911 if something happened." Peggy snickered.

"I'll do my best to avoid needing to make that call. Do you two have any plans for tomorrow?"

Both of my friends nodded their agreement. Since we were already at Mom's, we spent the rest of the day cleaning out old magazines and empty butter tubs. Peggy found a few quilting magazines. She poked them into her tote, with my permission. I gathered a small collection of family memorabilia and spread them out on the bed. My brother and I could sort them out later. I looked around the room and noticed a box of old greeting cards from friends on her dresser. I started to throw them into the trashcan, but noticed a few of them also contained that double B butterfly hidden in a tiny corner of the art. One of the cards had a date shortly after my college graduation, located below the double B signature. Now I had sure evidence that Bea had worked for the company for a while.

~~~~~

The heat blasted us as we stepped from the Rock and Roll Hall of Fame. I fanned myself with my bag of postcards.

"Those rockers sure were small. I think I'm too tall to fit into even the biggest costume we saw today. At least I found a tee-shirt that fits me." Marla hugged her shopping bag to her chest and grinned. She pulled out a torn tee shirt with a picture of the museum.

Peggy snorted. "I only got souvenirs for the grandkids. I don't think I'd want to be seen wearing that holey shirt if the ambulance came to get me. I could always put a layer of quilting behind all those tears in your shirt."

"Hey, rips and tears are the latest fashion these days." Marla started to dance and would have fallen if I hadn't grabbed her arm. We continued to chat about the guitars and costumes until we reached our parking spot on a side road near the museum.

I plugged Bea's last address into my phone and the GPS directed us out of the business part of downtown Cleveland and into an older neighborhood. As we drove down Kimberly Avenue, we saw a small crowd gathered around a house with a Superman symbol on the front.

Marla shouted, "Stop."

I pulled over to park on the side of the road. Marla jumped from the car as soon as I parked and joined the group reading the comics pasted to a metal fence. Peggy and I stepped closer to the others, moments after I locked the car. I perused the comics and
~~~~~

information attached to the fence. The house was the home of Jerry Siegel when he and Joe Shuster created Superman during their high school years. Bea and I once created a comic strip for the high school paper. I wrote the words and she did the drawings. I should have kept in contact with her. Who knows, we might have written a book together. I'd written a few unpublished things for my school kids. Maybe I should get them out again. It would be super if we could find Bea and have her illustrate my stories.

I stepped away from the gaggle and walked further down the block. The house where Bea lived should be nearby. What I found made a wave of disappointment wash over me. Boards covered the windows, tall grass filled the yard, and a condemned sign made note of a date for destruction. Bea no longer lived near Superman. But my Lois Lane genes were kicking in. I needed to find out who had stolen my friend's identity. Were they holding her somewhere and forcing her to illustrate and author books, while they took all the glory? I took a snapshot of the old place on my phone and headed back to Marla and Peggy, my steps filled with determination. Once I got to my friends, I asked the person sitting on Superman's porch about the neglected building.

"Nobody's lived there for as long as I've been around here, unless you count the vagrants that started a fire in the place a few years ago."

"Did you ever hear of an artist named Bea Bidwell? She lived there at one time."

"Some of the old folks used to call it the Bidwell-McDuffy house. Though, I never heard the name Bea associated with the place. I think the Smiths owned it, last I heard. They let the renters tear the place apart. It used to be a nice house." The woman paused. Her eyes narrowed into a squint. "Maybe this artist person has a website. Have you thought about looking for them on the internet?"

I hated to admit that I hadn't. I pulled out my phone and stabbed in Bea's name. She had a site, one without pictures of herself. Another dead end...

"Are you okay, honey? I can get you a bottle of water for two bucks."

I shook my head at the enterprising entrepreneur and herded my friends back to the car where I had a cooler full of bottled water.

I plugged in my home address and we headed north to connect with I-90 West. Before reaching the highway, we stopped to take pictures of each other with the official historical marker for the creators of Superman. We'd had a super day as far as sightseeing, but when it came to clues, we were crash, boom, zap, out of luck, as they say in comic books.

~~~~~

After sleeping in the next morning, I decided to explore Bea Bidwell's website a little more. After looking at the fine print, I finally located a place to leave a message.

> *Dear Bea,*
>
> *You may not remember me, but we were good friends from first grade until you left town to go to college. I saw that you've become a picture book illustrator. I always admired your drawings during our school years. It's fantastic to see that the rest of the world can now enjoy your talents. Did you recently speak at The Mazza Museum's annual conference? I missed it this year, but heard you were around.*

I struggled with how to delicately mention the perfect hand without offending her. Maybe I should be a little sneakier and ask her if she remembered the name of our old math teacher, the one that I had a picture of, with her iconic initials.

> *I'm happy to see you are still using your bee signature on your art. I still have one of your drawings from junior high math. I wondered if you remembered that teacher's name. Can you still recite his ode? We had such fun times that year. Please reply if you remember me.*
>
> *Sincerely,*
> *JoAnn Bartholomew*

I knew neither of us would ever forget Mr. Hitchcock's name. Not only had she drawn pictures, we'd also made up a cheer about him. I could still chant the piece. Only the real Bea would know his name for sure, since I hadn't mentioned what grade we had the guy. We only had math together one year in junior high. I'd have to wait for an answer. The information on the site said to wait up to a week.
~~~~~

I fixed a brunch of cinnamon toast and eggs. Mom had made that kind of breakfast when I invited school friends for an overnighter. I'm sure Bea probably enjoyed that treat more than once. I didn't meet Marla and Peggy until after my studies at college. They'd arrived in town when I finished my education and latched onto the jobs they'd held throughout long careers. We met when they started attending the church I grew up attending. We made it through Sunday school classes for singles, young married couples, and all the way to the seniors' class. I wish Bea had stayed in town so she could know my other friends. I wondered if she had buddies of her own or if she continued to go to church. She'd always been too shy for her own good, which made me even more curious about the person who'd presented to hundreds of teachers, authors, and illustrators at the conference.

A short time later, my phone rang. The secretary from The Mazza Museum let me know that she'd found a few photos of the person claiming to be Bea. She agreed to scan them and send the pictures my way. The images were fuzzy at best, unidentifiable at the worst. When I took out a magnifying glass, the imposter appeared to have all their hand-related digits and perfectly working arms on both sides.

"Did you get any videos back yet?" I tried to keep any annoyance out of my voice, but the woman sounded a little irritated when she answered to the negative. I thanked her profusely and tried to soothe her ire the best I could over the phone. I also promised to put in some extra volunteer hours over the next few weeks. She seemed happier after I agreed to be at the welcome desk the next afternoon, since the regularly scheduled greeter cancelled.

~~~~~

Sitting at the welcome desk the following day gave me more time to inspect the plaster hand of the supposed Bea Bidwell. It looked like a perfectly formed left hand with a large wedding band encircling the ring finger. If this was Bea, why hadn't she changed to a married name? Besides, the Bea I knew wrote and drew using her right hand. I flipped through the biography notebook again and read through the details. The description included brief information about the illustrator growing up in my hometown and graduating from my high school. It mentioned the art school where my friend had gone when we parted ways. My teeth ground
~~~~~

together. I almost screamed my thoughts about the imposter aloud, but a family entered the museum doors.

I put on a welcoming smile and told them about the museum's galleries with different themes. They could take time to explore the picture books, illustrator biography notebooks, and check out the original art hanging on the walls. I explained that the exhibits changed periodically due to the museum owning a huge collection locked away in a sealed room. If they came again, chances were they'd be able to see something different with each visit. They lingered for a while in the first gallery, admiring the plaster hands. One of them spotted the hand holding a dog's paw. I walked over and showed them the book about the dog. I opened to the page with a plastic tab and held it up by the displayed art. After that, I left them to explore the rest of the museum on their own.

My thoughts returned to Bea. She'd always enjoyed playing with our dog, Bessie. Her father had been allergic to animals, so our dog was her only pet experience. I hoped she had another pet at some time in her life. Bessie loved having her over for a fun game of fetch. I walked back over to her display and picked up Bea's picture book. As I perused the story and art, I paused and studied the dog that seemed to appear in the background on each page, telling his own story. The long floppy ears and orange spots reminded me of my old hound that had befriended Bea. Something was definitely rotten in Picture Book Land.

When the family touring the museum finally left, I pulled out my phone and called Mom at the retirement home. Hopefully she would not be off playing BINGO. Games had never been her forte in the past, but now that she had started a new phase in life, they'd become appealing.

"Hi, JoAnn. I'm getting ready to go down for a sing-a-long in the great room, so make it snappy."

"I love you too, Mom. Look, I'm going to stop by after I'm done at Mazza. Could you try to remember a few things about my friend, Bea Bidwell? I'm doing a little research on her and need your perspective."

"I'll try. You know I have my good and bad days about remembering everything."

"Don't worry, I'll take what you can give and be satisfied." Some days I thought Mom had a better recollection of things than I did. "Have fun singing."

"You know I will." Mom led singing at their church until a younger praise band took over. I was glad her new home included music as part of their activities.

No one else came through the museum that day. I had time to pull out my phone and snap a few pictures of Bea's display. I'd share my findings with Marla and Peggy at the coffee shop tomorrow morning. We had a standing breakfast date to discuss the latest happenings for each week. I had plenty to share.

~~~~~

"So, what did your mother remember about Bea?" Peggy stabbed her fork into an oversized omelet.

"Her memories of Bea were hazy, but she recalled some important details about Mr. and Mrs. Bidwell that may help us solve this case." I paused dramatically. Both my friends stopped sipping their coffees. Peggy rolled one hand in a circle, suggesting I continue.

Marla was a little blunter. "Spill it, girl. Don't hold us in suspense."

"Bea's parents kept in contact with mine after they retired and moved away. They had a beautiful cabin in the woods near a creek, according to Lucille Bidwell's letters to Mom. Their house number was easy to recall. They said it was God's perfect number, twelve. The street was Cat Tail Bottoms Road, which made Mom giggle when she remembered it. She couldn't recall the name of the town or city, but I did an internet search last night and found the road near Anna, Ohio. It looks like the cabin is now in Bea's name."

Marla whipped out her clue notebook and jotted down the address as a mysterious grin spread across her face. "Anna. Interesting. So what should we do with this information?"

Peggy placed both hands on the table, making the silverware rattle. "I think we should do a stakeout and case the place."

Those were my thoughts exactly. "Are you two ready for another road trip? The location is less than two hours away."

They both agreed. We quickly finished our breakfast and returned to our homes to pack snacks, bring binoculars, and collect whatever we needed for a long day of spying. We decided to take Marla's dark brown sedan instead of my red compact SUV. It would be less conspicuous, according to Marla, who rarely wanted
~~~~~

to drive her car when we went on trips together. I found that quite intriguing but decided not to complain.

We chatted the whole way there about our plans to spy on either my friend, or the imposter who had taken over her life. I secretly hoped the address would lead us to Bea so we could let her know what we had discovered. Then we could work together to bring justice to the imposter. When we got near the exit for Anna, we all took a break at a rest park to stretch our legs and use the facilities. Age had a way of catching up with our bodies if we didn't stop for breaks. Marla grabbed a couple of pamphlets and seemed to be studying them.

Once we were off the highway, Marla wove the car through the streets of Anna. I wondered if our driver had lost her way. She assured me that she knew her destination. Then, she suddenly hit the brake hard enough to tighten the seatbelt across my chest. An excited squeal came from the driver's seat.

"Whoa, did an animal run in front of you?" I grabbed the arm rest to settle back into my seat.

"There's the historical marker for a Newberry Award winning book. I knew we'd go by it eventually. I have to stop and take a look." Marla pulled into the parking lot of a library and jumped from the car like a hound in pursuit of a rabbit. She shouted back to us as she pointed at the sign. "Look, it's the marker for Lois Lenski. Her *Strawberry Girl* was one of my favorite books as a child. It was also the story that won the award."

Peggy and I followed her at a more sedate pace, until we stood in front of a plaque honoring Lois Lenski, who also illustrated her own books. I knew an answered prayer when I saw it. "You know, if you volunteer at the Mazza you might see some of her illustrations in person." My comment seemed to fall on deaf ears as the former librarian studied the front and back of the author/illustrator's marker. Peggy seemed too busy stretching her neck and muttering something about getting whiplash. After Marla's moment of fiction fandom drew to an end, we hopped back into the car with the assurance that we were heading directly toward our intended destination.

Fields of corn and occasional forested areas lined the sides of the country road we traveled, for several miles. Marla slowed, this time gently, and turned down a narrow road leading into trees. A creek meandered alongside the pavement. We slowly cruised down Cat Tail Bottoms Road, passing several nice-looking cabins. The path dead ended at a small public boat ramp, not far from the address I had memorized.

"Let's park the car here. We can pretend we're out for a walk and see if we can spot your friend, or the imposter." Marla let out a cleansing breath. She'd driven for longer than I'd ever seen her do before.

"I'll be ready to make the call if we need the authorities." Peggy waved her phone in the air as she stepped from the car, shouldering her quilted bag.

I checked my cell and noted only one little dot in the connection icon. I doubted we'd get much help from a phone call, but didn't want to disillusion my friend.

We were on our own.

We had nothing to fear, hopefully.

I pulled Dad's battered gray fishing hat over my curls. I missed the old guy, but I was glad to have somewhat of a disguise. Peggy's neon green sunhat and Marla's hot pink visor did little to keep us camouflaged. I muttered a quiet prayer for our safety as we headed out. We passed by the suspect's cabin going up the road. No one came out.

We walked to the end of Cat Tail Bottoms Road and then turned around to make our way back. There were several places that looked like log cabins. A few had white siding or brick instead of logs. The one supposedly owned by my friend looked like it had been sided with large stones. I gawked at the place as we made our way by again. I forgot to look where I was going and tripped into Marla's backside. We both fell to the ground in a tangle, shrieking as we went down.

Peggy bent over us. "Are you two all right? Can you tell me where you hurt?" Her experience as a former 911 operator kicked in as she tried to assess our status using a strong voice. Between her loud questions and our squawking, we made enough noise to get the attention of the surrounding neighborhood. This wasn't the way I planned to call Bea's imposter out, but the front door of the rock-covered house opened. Two very similar looking women stepped out onto the porch and headed our way. An older man pushed a walker down the driveway across the street. I wanted to hide, but the earth didn't open up and swallow me whole. I brushed my hands off as best I could and stood to face my friend's predicament.

Marla sat on the ground, rubbing her ankle. Her eyes grew big when the two women got closer. Peggy's eyes did the same after she finished inspecting Marla's injury and turned their way. In harmony they both exclaimed, "Twins?"

One of the women laughed. "We get that all the time, but we are only cousins." She waved a hand between them. "I am Georgia McDuffy and this is my cousin..."

"Bea Bidwell, my old friend." I finished the woman's sentence then turned accusing eyes her way. "What I want to know is why you came to the Mazza Conference and impersonated Bea. Are you holding her hostage and stealing her talent?"

"Is everything all right, ladies?" A lower voice broke into our conversation. I'd forgotten about the man from across the way.

Bea waved her hand, the one I knew so well, with the missing fingers. "Everything is fine, Mr. Berkshire. An old friend of mine has come to visit and took a tumble with her companion. Georgia and I will take them inside and get our first aid kit."

I bit my tongue and held onto my unanswered questions as we lifted Marla from the ground. Mr. Berkshire offered her the use of a cane that he'd carried in his walker's basket. She took it with a promise to leave it with Bea. He headed for his home. The rest of us made an awkward parade as we hobbled our way up to Bea's cabin. I sidled up to my old friend and took her elbow in mine. "Are you safe?"

She giggled. The sound took me back to our shared childhood memories. "Of course, you silly kickapoo."

I relaxed. The word had been a code between us at one time, meaning all was well. "So what is going on with your cousin impersonating you?"

"Hush, we need to talk about this inside. Mr. Berkshire may look old, but he still has pretty good hearing. He also has quite a mouth for gossiping."

Once we'd had our wounds cleaned and bandaged, I looked at the two women and demanded to know what was going on.

Bea cleared her throat and began talking. "After college I moved into a house in Cleveland with my cousin Georgia and her husband to save money. She had a degree in public relations. I worked for a greeting card company. Eventually I started landing contracts for illustrating."

Georgia took over the conversation. "She was really good. Eventually the publishers wanted her to start doing public appearances to promote the books. Bea felt really self-conscious about her birth defects and asked me to stand in for her. My husband had passed. I needed something to do. I loved talking about her work and we looked so alike that most people didn't notice the difference. She never appeared in public if she could avoid it. I tried to limit the number of times I took her place."

"But wouldn't the disability be something the publishers would want to play up? Today it seems like that is something that might be a good publicity approach. When I worked as a librarian, we were encouraged to find out special things about authors. It is helpful for needy children to see those who have overcome something that might have held them back." Marla shifted her ankle as it sat on a cushioned stool.

"I wanted people to enjoy my work because of its quality, not because of my deformity." Bea stuck out a stubborn chin. I'd seen that expression when we were kids and someone tried to feel sorry for her.

I squirmed in my seat. "I see your point, but it isn't right that the plaster cast of Georgia's hand is on display with your art at The Mazza Museum. Think of other people who might be inspired to do works of art, despite issues with their hands."

Georgia's head nodded in agreement, along with everyone else's in the room. "I told you so. I felt really bad about allowing them to use my hand. I even called home to see if she'd change her mind, but Bea told me to go ahead. My dead husband is probably rolling over in his grave that we've been so deceitful. He died early, bless his soul. Not too long after he passed, we started our little scheme. I had quit my job to take care of my baby. I kept the Cleveland house for a while. Then we all moved into this little cabin when Bea inherited it. She made a wonderful aunt and helped support both of us through my daughter's early years."

Peggy laid a comforting hand on Georgia's wrist. "Where is your daughter now?"

"Leah lives a few miles away from here. She married a local

farmer, and they have a couple of toddlers. I hope she never goes to The Mazza and discovers our deception. We brought her up to be a good Christian woman. I don't think she will understand what we've done. We were so careful to keep the truth from her over the years. I'm tired of carrying that burden." Georgia wiped a tear from her cheeks and looked steadily at her cousin.

Bea closed her eyes as the room grew quiet. She huffed out a chest full of air and looked down at her hands as tears leaked from her own eyes. "May God and everyone we've led astray forgive us for what we've done. We will start by going to the museum and making things right. I'm sorry I hid my disability for so long."

~~~~~

A month later, Marla, Peggy, and I toured the Hands On Display, along with the new docent recruits. I turned and looked at my class. "When you give a tour of this display there are several interesting things for the students to look for. One is the hand which is also holding a dog's paw. Another is the one with the bloody finger. This display for Bea Bidwell's work is special to me. She and I attended school together. Despite her disability, she is able to create beautiful illustrations for children's books."

I couldn't help the smile that spread across my face. Bea sent one of my stories to her publisher. One day, I would have my own picture book illustrated by my friend. Forcing my thoughts back to the present, I asked, "Does anyone have any comments or questions?"

"Showing the children that they can overcome problems in their life is important. Bea's art would be a great way to start a conversation about doing your best, even if you aren't perfect." Marla smiled at me as she shared her idea.

"Don't forget to mention that blood on the plaster has a rust color after it has dried. I know this because some of my quilts have brown spots from where I poked my finger." Peggy grinned. The rest of the group groaned as she shared more knowledge about bloody things.

Tours this year were going to be very interesting, very interesting indeed.

END
~~~~~

Literary places mentioned in this story:

The Mazza Museum is located on the University of Findlay campus, Findlay, Ohio. The idea of having a museum of original picture book illustrations started with the donation of four pieces of art, given by the Mazza family to the college's library. Through donations, by artists, works bought by donors, and museum purchases, the museum has grown to over 20,000 pieces of art in over forty years. Approximately 300 pieces are on rotating displays while a vault protects the rest of the extensive collection from the elements. The museum is under great professional leadership, but it relies heavily on volunteer docents, museum hostesses, behind-the-scenes helpers, library aides, and bookstore workers. Touring the museum is free to the public and the facility provides educational packets to teachers. The Mazza is a popular destination for school field trips offering museum tours, an art class, STEAM activities in their new Science/Technology/ Engineering/Arts/Math Lab, and visits to the on-campus planetarium. The author of this story volunteers as a docent for school field trips.

The creators of superhero Superman birthed their idea when they lived in Cleveland, Ohio. Jerry Siegel and Joe Shuster went to high school in the area when they started working together to create their 'man of steel.' Their ideas inspired others to create comic book heroes that have become a whole different type of literary industry. A historical marker located in their old neighborhood honors their work. Jerry Siegel's home still exists in the area.

Ohio author and illustrator, Lois Lenski, is honored with a marker near the Anna, Ohio library. As a child she lived in the area and was inspired by her time there to write and illustrate books about rural historical children. Strawberry Girl won the Newberry Award and she had two other books that received honors from that award.

In the main branch of the Toledo Lucas County Library there is a room dedicated to Nancy Drew. It is found in their extensive children's library. One of the main ghost writers for the series was Millie Benson. She was a longtime reporter for the Toledo Blade, in addition to writing for the series. The room contains copies of her books, games about Nancy Drew, paintings from book covers, and other memorabilia.

About the Author:

Bettie Boswell has always loved to read and write. That interest helped her create musicals for both church and school, and eventually she decided to write and illustrate stories to share with the world. Her writing interests extend from children's to adult and from fiction to non-fiction. She has two published novels, Free to Love and On Cue. In addition to writing novels, she has written other works including leveled readers, magazine articles, and has contributed to lesson plan collections, devotionals, and short story anthologies. There are publication plans for a picture book and chapter book in 2023. She is a minister's wife, church musician, mother of two grown men, and a grandma to three. She loves the arts and shares her doodles, and photography from her daily walks, on social media.

BOVINE
By JPC Allen

Yes. Yes.

Fingering my sideburn, I scanned the miniscule living room. The mixture of search and destruction was quite similar to that found in the apartment of my agent after his robbery three years ago.

Seat cushions, some ripped open, lay scattered on the hardwood floor with tossed books interspersed among them. Lamps overturned. A glass-topped table shattered.

I inhaled deeply.

Odd. I hadn't expected staging a crime scene to bring out the artist in me. Although all my efforts were probably wasted on the audience for which I had prepared it.

The reason I'd asked Sara to stay at her writer's retreat for a few weeks was because law enforcement in such a forsaken county of this forsaken state had to be mediocre at best. From what I had learned through my research of the police presence in Marlin County, Ohio, the officers could trip over a body with a suicide note pinned to the shirt and still mull over the possibility of murder.

I shoved a DVD player into a large garbage bag with other "stolen" items I had collected from around the house. I lifted the small TV from the stand by the fireplace and walked up the three steps to the eat-in kitchen. On the mat by the back door, I removed the cheap tennis shoes that had allowed every ounce of moisture from the drenched ground to freeze my feet as I had tromped out a fake trail from the cabin to the crumbling stretch of pavement passing as a road. I slipped into my own waterproof boots and let myself out the back door. Since I was renting Sara's rustic getaway, concern for fingerprints was unwarranted.

I turned up my collar to the chilly late October rain that had spat from the sky every day since I'd exiled myself to this cursed county. Taking a rag I'd found in a small outbuilding, I wrapped my fist and punched out the glass pane in the door that was nearest the knob. The shards tinkled on the linoleum—who besides the destitute used linoleum anymore?

Then I added the rag to the contents of the bag, along with the tennis shoes and a pair of bargain-basement boots, which I had worn to give the illusion of two thieves.

With the TV under one arm and juggling my flashlight in the hand that also held the bag, I crossed the stone pavers that Sara considered a patio and struck out across the sodden grass to the crest of the hill on which the little house sat.

Sara found this place inspirational? An idyllic oasis? I knew the poor girl couldn't entirely shed her provincial roots—eighteen was simply too late to move to New York and go native. But she always projected a charming sincerity in her efforts to overcome her background. Sincere but completely useless.

I stopped at the top of the slope. This would be tricky with my hands full. Testing each step for solidity, I picked my way down the steep descent, slick from a disgusting combination of decomposing leaves and mud. Achieving the bottom without mishap, I played my light along the bank of a creek roaring with excessive rainfall.

Where was that hole?

Tense minutes bounded by and then the beam revealed the hole I'd dug this afternoon. I dropped the sack in the hole, something breaking on contact with the ground, and dumped the TV on top of it, which also gave a resounding crack.

A pity for Sara, but she must have been insured.

I heaped mud over the objects and then, using the shovel as a lever, I rolled a rotted log onto the disturbed earth, nearly rupturing my diaphragm.

To prevent a fall, I climbed up the endless hill with the shovel as a steadying aid and employed it to obliterate my tracks to the hole. How could Sara own this property and not bother to install proper paths?

After leaving the shovel in the outbuilding, I entered by the back door, removed my boots and went to what was supposed to be the master bedroom but was far too small to earn that appellation. I changed into dry clothes and carried my wet garments to the washer.

I departed the house by the front door and trotted down the stone steps embedded in the small hill that ran down to the drive. From behind the wheel of the decrepit rental sedan, I gazed up at the one-story, log cabin horror built from pseudo logs. The boredom from staying here almost negated the value of my plan.

Almost.

I backed down the lengthy rutted path that Sara had the temerity to christen a drive and turned onto the county road. Unwilling to take the hairpin turns at more than 25 mph for fear of meeting my demise at the bottom of a ravine, I crawled to a little white church on a ridge.

I opened my phone. Yes, it received reception. Once I'd discovered how spotty the internet service was in Marlin County, I had no confidence of being connected to the civilized world when I needed to be.

Inhaling in rapid succession to achieve a panicky sound, I dialed 911.

"911. What is the address of your emergency?"

"I've been robbed," I gasped, tinging my voice with fear. "This is Harrison Sharpe. I'm staying at Sara Novak's vacation home. I saw two men run out of the house, carrying heavy loads."

~~~~~

The fall rain had transformed into a torrent by the time an SUV from the sheriff's department finally pulled into the parking lot. If robbers had actually broken into the house, they would have had time to finish several beers before the police appeared.

An officer came to my door, and I lowered the window, allowing the rain to pour in.

"Mr. Sharpe?" said the young deputy, shining his flashlight at my face.

"Were you expecting a crowd here at this time of night?" I said. "Please lower your light. I only have two eyes."

The deputy aimed the beam at my chest. "I'm sorry, sir." He was the officer who looked Latino, but I'd learned his last name was Kincaid. "You told dispatch you saw someone running from your rental home."

"I saw two someones." I repeated my story of seeing two men fleeing from the house against the illumination of a floodlight.

"I'll go check it out. You can follow me."
~~~~~

The roads were empty along the entirety of our trip.

At the foot of the drive, another police SUV was parked, headlights piercing the filthy dark, windshield wipers working. A hulking figure lumbered toward us.

The deputy exited his SUV, and both people walked back to me.

Although I would be soaked, I had to let down my window again.

"Mr. Sharpe," the young deputy said, "have you met Sheriff Malinowski?"

So my call had rated an appearance by the Blond Ox himself.

"Just call me Mal." The towering giant offered a hand similar in width to a platter.

How quaint. Upon our first meeting, I was already allowed to call a local official by his nickname. I took the platter. "Harrison Sharpe."

"Oh, I know who you are, Mr. Sharpe. Just about everybody in the county knew you were renting Ms. Novak's place within a couple of hours of you crossing the county line."

Unquestionably gratifying. My reputation as a novelist and essayist had penetrated this backwater of Ohio.

"Kincaid and I will check out the house," said the Ox. "When it's safe, we'll come back and get you."

They vanished into the woods that grew in utter abandon along both sides of the road and driveway.

My rental car was in danger of running out of gas when they returned.

The Ox pecked on my window, forcing me, once again, to lower it and receive another shower. "The place has been ransacked," he said.

"Do you think it was addicts?" I said in a hushed voice.

"Possibly. But it could have been anyone who needed cash fast and didn't want to work for it."

Meaning the Ox had most of the population of this county and all the neighboring ones to put on his list of suspects. Excellent.

He said, "You'll have to tell us what, if anything, is missing."

"I'll try." I raised the window as much as I could. "But I can only be certain of my own belongings. This is the first time I've stayed at Sara's house. I am unfamiliar with what she keeps here."

The rental heap rocked through the ruts on the driveway, and I parked at the foot of the stone steps. The sheriff led me to the small front porch, held the door open for me, and then followed me from room to room as I made a pretense of examining the spaces for missing items.

The Ox would nod and note any item I thought might be stolen.

There wasn't any other way to think of the man. Most people in this wasteland had some aspect of the bovine, but "Mal" was the epitome—six inches above my six feet, shoulders like a beast of burden, and a dull, placid expression in his blue eyes. When my research revealed he led a department of eight officers and that he was under forty, serving his first term as sheriff, Fate had served me the perfect location for my scheme.

Once our tour was complete, we returned to the living room.

"Nothing of yours is missing?" The Ox leafed through his notes.

"Correct. I'm very fortunate. I took my computer and phone with me to the Thurber House in Columbus. I'm conducting research for an article."

"I heard about that. You're writing an article on the literary heritage of Ohio."

"Yes." I implanted that word with as much fake enthusiasm as it could hold. "I pitched the idea of a series of articles about various states' contributions to national, and even international, literature to an editor friend of mine. She thought it brilliant and told me to send her the first installment. When I remembered Sara owned this cabin in her home state, I decided to start here. It's quite easy to do the research. Your state has created a map called the Ohio Literary Trail."

Ingenious cover story. Writers can go anywhere and claim they are in their present location for research purposes. I had to have a better excuse than a vacation when all my friends knew my taste in that area ran to Dubai and Monaco.

The Ox said, "I need Ms. Novak's number." Then he frowned, staring at the fireplace with its hodge-podge pattern of heavy stones. "That's funny. Since all the items but the TV were very small, you'd think they'd've gone for those."

He stepped around a disemboweled cushion and broken lamp,

staring at two flintlock pistols hanging on hooks above the mantle.

"They're fake," I said. "Sara told me that because she didn't want me to think she kept unsecured firearms on the premises. I have no idea why she owns them. I'm sure she can afford the real thing. I suppose the thieves could tell."

"I don't know how, just by looks." The Ox lifted one gun from its hook. "But you can by holding them. They're too light."

"Then they must have grabbed them and put them back." I coughed to cover a smile.

Inferring that most of the male rednecks would possess a deep knowledge of firearms, I had decided leaving the guns in place would bolster the illusion of locals being responsible for the crime.

The deputy entered through the front door. "Can't find any more tracks. They seem to stop at the road. A third person may have been waiting for them or they parked their car on the side of the road."

"Tracks?" I said.

"Yes, sir. Two distinct sets—one perp appears to have worn boots, the other tennis shoes. The tracks come up from the road, through the woods to the back door and then go back through the woods almost the same way, but this time, running."

After getting soaked to the skin, I was glad he'd noticed all the fine details I had applied to the tracks.

The Ox turned to me, "Did you pass any vehicles on the road before you turned onto the drive?"

"Not that I recall. But it's such a rotten night that I doubt I would have noticed another car unless it was coming straight at me."

"Was the alarm going off when you saw the suspects?"

"I don't know. I think I would have heard it even from inside my car. I set the alarm. Or at least, I tried to. It's rather complicated." I gasped. "Do you think I didn't set it correctly and the thieves broke in undetected?"

"Very likely. We'll have to check with the security firm, but it appears the alarm wasn't set."

Shaking my head, I sighed. "What a stupid mistake. I owe Sara an apology."

"Wait until I check with the firm." The Ox poised his pencil over his notepad. "Ms. Novak's number?"

I gave it to him. He asked if I wanted to stay in the house with the back door unsecured.

Pitching my voice higher, I said, "Do you think they'll return?"

"No. I'd be stunned if they did."

I deduced it took very little to stun the Ox.

He went on, "Except for your electronics, it looks like they took anything that was worth anything. But I'll have to check with Ms. Novak." He closed his pad. "If it would ease your mind, I can station Kincaid here for the rest of his shift. But if he gets a call, he'll have to leave. I'm sure the lodge at the state park will have rooms available since it's so late in October."

Pretending to be nervous was acceptable; acting cowardly was decidedly not. "Thank you, sheriff. I'll be fine. I'd appreciate the deputy staying as long as he is able."

The two officers departed.

I pushed the kitchen table against the back door — must play the part of worried victim.

Then I picked up the receiver for the landline — the only means of communication to the outside world from this hole — and dialed Ariella's number. She had better answer.

After three rings, she did. "I'm not coming out there, Harrison," she said, annoyance marring her rich contralto. "Our marriage is over. Get used to it."

I heaved a sigh. "I can't bring myself to think that. But I called to say that you shouldn't come at present."

"Oh." Extended pause.

Models aren't known for their sterling intellects.

"Why the change in tune, Harrison? You've spent the past week begging me to come, telling me how perfect Sara's place is for us to reconcile."

"It is. I'm convinced we need to get away from our lawyers and jobs and friends and focus on us. But — well, something has happened." I explained the circumstances of the robbery.

"The sheriff thinks it's safe, but what does he know? He seems more suited to moving hay bales than investigating crimes. Besides, I should have the door fixed and make absolutely certain the security system is working properly before you come. That may take some time." I sighed again. "I miss you."

"It's taken you six months to miss me."

"Getting away from the stress of our lives in New York has helped me see what's most important to me—you and our marriage."

"Oh." Another eon of a pause. "That's very thoughtful of you, Harrison. I didn't expect that from you."

"I've changed, Ari. Entirely."

We chatted a few minutes more, and I ended the conversation with a promise to call back if I thought it was safe for her to join me.

Hanging up, I smiled.

She was weakening.

~~~~~

Honestly, why had they bothered putting this tiny exhibit on their literary trail? If Zane Grey wasn't important enough as an author to earn his own, exclusive museum but had to be linked to one about the history of the National Road—whatever that was— he obviously should have been omitted from their map.

I viewed with utter disinterest the museum's recreation of the author's study. I had to continue the charade of researching literary sites in this benighted state to maintain my cover and have some accurate information if anyone asked me how my research was progressing. Relying solely on the internet seemed a probable way to ruin the illusion of the writer hard at work.

Glancing at my phone, I headed for the entrance. Ten minutes, plus photos, was more than enough time to speak knowingly about this place.

I had nearly reached the double doors when someone called my name.

I surveyed my immediate surroundings. Who would know me here?

"Mr. Sharpe." A tall, slender woman in her thirties with flaming hair approached me in breathless haste. "Didn't you find what you were looking for? I saw you walk in. The staff is very helpful and knowledgeable if you need specific information for your article."

Drawing to my full height, which often had the very pleasant effect of making unwanted interlocutors feel microscopic, I said, "You have the advantage of me."

"Oh, I'm sorry." She held out a slim hand. "I'm Jeanine Norris. I write as Jim Norris."
~~~~~

A dim recollection of a conversation with a loquacious cashier at a disheveled grocery store rose in my memory. "You live in Marlin County," I said. "When someone mentioned there was a local author of mysteries, she didn't explain that Jim Norris is a woman."

"My initials before I got married were J, I, and M, so I thought it'd be fun to write as Jim Norris." She grinned. "It's my secret identity."

The only compliment I could credit to this woman was that she didn't appear as thoroughly bovine as her fellow citizens. A modicum of intelligence registered in her over-sized blue eyes. It must have been the literary nature of her work. If mysteries qualified as literature.

I said, "Your pseudonym, I'm sure, amply protects you from your hordes of devoted fans who would trample a trail to your door if they discovered where your home was located."

She laughed. "I don't think I have enough fans to make one full horde." Her hand fluttered toward the main room of the museum. "Were you looking for something in particular?"

Why was this any business of hers? I needed time to concoct an answer.

I turned the table. "Why are you here?"

"I'm doing research for a new series of historical mysteries, set in Ohio during the early 1800s."

Inspiration, as usual, ignited. "My readers wouldn't be interested in Zane Grey."

"Really? He was very successful." Her quiet voice grew eager. "His novel *Riders of the Purple Sage* was filmed—"

"Please." I held up a hand to stem the flood of useless information. "My articles appeal to highly educated urbanites and suburbanites. An author of westerns from a hundred years ago won't interest them." I pulled out my phone, pretending it had pinged. "I have to take this."

I hurried into the parking lot, slammed into the rental wreck, and dialed Ariella.

"Hello, Harrison." She positively cooed.

She was coming. But I couldn't sound like I knew.

"Hello, lover. I really don't want to pester you, but have you given my request any more thought? The security firm gave the alarm system a clean bill of health. The thieves must not have triggered it the night of the robbery because I didn't set it correctly. And I spoke to Sara. She's never had any trouble in the six years she's owned the house. I think it's safe. And…" dramatic pause "… life is so empty without you."

She whispered, "I miss you, too."

I smirked. A glimpse in the rearview mirror revealed that the expression was not flattering, especially for someone with classically handsome features. But I could not restrain myself.

She actually missed my money. Six months was enough time for her to discover that it was far easier to access it by remaining married to me than fighting for it in divorce court.

"I already booked a flight." She gave me the day and time.

"You've realized my fondest hopes, Ari." Suppressing my natural loathing for the hovel, I said, "You'll love Sara's house. It's just the place for us to remember why we fell in love."

~~~~~

"It's absolutely gorgeous, Harrison." Ariella continued to turn the tennis bracelet of diamonds and sapphires set in platinum, the faint light from the dashboard making the facets gleam.

"As soon as I saw it, I knew you'd love it. Consider it a peace offering."

A tractor—a tractor!—crept along the road in front of us, and I pummeled the horn.

Ari studied the jewelry with the open-mouthed fascination of a child. It didn't take much to fascinate Ari, especially when she knew the price tag.

The lodge and conference center at the state park—they actually had the gall to name the jumble of timbers that—appeared through the steady drizzle as we rounded a tight bend in the road. Although October had turned to November, the new month proved as wet as the old.

I pulled into a parking space, and Ari placed her finely manicured hand on the latch of the door.

I took hold of her other one. "I don't mind driving to Columbus for dinner. The food here barely qualifies as fodder."

"So sweet." Ari gave me a quick peck on the lips. "But I'm still tired from traveling yesterday. Besides, it will give us more time to be alone at the house."
~~~~~

Clamping my teeth together so they wouldn't grind, I exited the heap, raced round to Ari's door, and opened it.

In the lobby, which couldn't decide if it was pretending to rustic chic or dilapidated shack, every head turned toward us.

Although twenty-five was well behind her, Ariella couldn't help attracting attention, even among the bovines. Slim, long-limbed, with a face that could launch hundreds of thousands of ships and had gained hundreds of thousands of social media followers, Ari wore her make-up and casual designer clothes exquisitely and moved to the doorway of the restaurant with the grace of a thoroughbred.

We were shown to a table by soaring windows. The young waitress I had had the last time I'd lowered myself to dine here approached and then faltered, her eyes fixing on me, obviously recalling who I was.

Dropping her gaze and slumping her shoulders, she trudged toward us.

I sat back in the uncomfortable chair. This was going to be fun. One should take advantage of any opportunities Fate offered to administer revenge.

"Good evening," she whispered. "Our specials tonight are--"

"Can you hear her, Ari?" I said. "I can't. Speak up. Act like you know what you're doing." I leaned toward her, locking my gaze on hers.

The girl stiffened, and I heard her swallow.

She told us the specials.

I made her repeat them.

She did, her voice growing fainter and more hesitant.

I peered at her name tag. "Claire, is it? I still can't tell what you're saying, Claire. I'll have to order from the menu." I snapped it open.

Ari ordered what was supposedly a steak dinner. I did the same but asked for several substitutes for the side dishes.

"Do you have that all written down?" I caught the waitress's frightened eyes.

Perhaps twenty and not ugly at all with buttery blond hair and a smooth, round face, but still unquestionably bovine.

"Yes, sir." She looked down at her pad.

"You'd better. I'd hate to have to talk to your manager."

Her head jerked in a nod, and she scuttled away.

"What did the kid do to you, Harrison?" Any trace of warmth in Ariella's voice had fled. "Or are you just in one of your nasty moods?"

"That girl humiliated me." The memory of that moment choked my words. "She spilled water on me the last time I was desperate enough to dine here, making me look ridiculous in front of everyone in the restaurant."

Ari slid the hand with the bracelet across the table and gripped mine. "I'm sure it was an accident. I want to enjoy our dinner. And you."

A retort fought to free itself from my lips, but I had to play the besotted husband. "Of course." I squeezed her elegant fingers. "Whatever you wish."

I behaved as Ari asked throughout our trial that the local yokels considered fine dining.

Ari chatted with the waitress, only too happy to show off her bracelet and to mention the $20,000 price with the subtlety of a strafing fighter jet. As we finished the slop we ordered for dessert, the waitress took my credit card.

The window to fully enact my revenge was closing.

Pushing aside the barely touched dish, I said, "If you need to touch up your make-up, lover, I'll wait for my credit card and meet you in the lobby."

Ariella kissed me and left the table. All the cattle lifted their heads from their feed, watching Ari as she crossed the restaurant with the poise that had conquered the runway.

Their appreciation was as satisfying as a slice of Kobe steak. They knew she was with me.

The waitress scurried to my table with my card in the folder.

Slipping my hand into my pocket, I fingered change, both bills and coins, because some people in this medieval hamlet insisted on cash.

I signed the receipt and handed it to her.

"The tip isn't on the card." I pulled out the coins and flung them on the floor. "There it is."

As the color draining away from her cheeks turned her pale complexion ghostly, I sailed out of the restaurant and into the lobby.

~~~~~

Who was knocking at this unholy hour? And why didn't Ari make him or her stop?

Hurling off the bed clothes, I whipped around to Ari and — she wasn't there.

Someone continued hammering "The Anvil Chorus."

Why didn't Ari answer the door?

Struggling into my bathrobe, I heard water running.

All right. She was very fortunate she had a legitimate excuse for forcing me out of bed and that I still had to pretend to be the pining spouse.

I marched to the front door and slammed it open, delivering my most withering glare.

The Blond Ox had his fist raised to knock again. "Are you all right, Mr. Sharpe?"

"Of course not." I knotted the belt of my cashmere robe. "Not when I'm rousted out of bed at dawn."

"It's after 11, sir. But I'm sorry if I disturbed you and your wife."

Perfectly natural for me to think it was shortly after daybreak. The leaden sky frustrated virtually all efforts of the sun to illuminate this damp corner of the planet.

"Your apology will be placed under review." I dismissed it with a flick of my hand. "What do you want?"

"I just wanted to go over your statement again. We haven't gotten — hello. You must be Mrs. Sharpe." He offered Ariella his platter of a hand.

Wearing a voluminous silk robe, she lowered the towel she was using to dry her cinnamon brown hair and gripped the platter, her bracelet glittering on her wrist. "Please. Call me Ariella. Are you the sheriff investigating the robbery? Harrison mentioned you."

She was using her sultry voice. Mere reflex. Ari flirted with any male from nine to ninety.

"Yes, ma'am. You can call me Mal." He watched her a moment. Perhaps her flirtatious tone had touched a nerve or maybe he thought he recognized her. "I just wanted to go over your husband's statement again, see if he'd remembered anything more about what he saw the night of the break-in."
~~~~~

"No leads?" I said.

He shook his head. "Nothing's been pawned yet."

"There's nothing more I can tell you. I only glimpsed the two men."

The Ox made me go over my story again, standing on the porch, taking notes, but his obtuse blue eyes kept straying over us while Ari and I remained in the open door. I didn't invite him in, sending the clear message to keep his visit as short as possible.

"Oh, sheriff—Mal." Ari gave her head a coquettish tilt. Another reflex. "Do you know where we can buy firewood? I'd love to have a real wood fire in the fireplace." She hugged my arm.

"But, lover," I said, "we don't know how to build a fire."

"It can't be that hard." Ari aimed a hopeful grin at the Ox.

He studied her—if he was capable of such a mental exercise—for the longest time, and then said, "I know a guy who—"

"I'm sure you know a guy for everything." I was rude, but the man had to leave. "Sara very thoughtfully provided a binder with phone numbers for local services. I just recalled that there's one listed for firewood, and it says to ask for Walter."

Why a surname wasn't included puzzled me, unless they were still considered a new-fangled invention, like forks. Perhaps he was simply known as Walter the Woodcutter.

The Ox continued to stare at us as if he hadn't heard a word I said. Then he pulled a knit hat over his blond crewcut. "I'll be walking the property again, see if we missed anything. Like some tracks."

Ari's posture perked to attention. "Tracks? What tracks?"

"We found two sets of tracks, ma'am," said the Ox. "One set of tennis shoes and one set of boots leading from the road to the back door and then back down to the road."

"Did you make—what do they call it, Harrison? Oh, casts! Did you make casts?"

"Yes, ma'am. But those only help us if those prints are found at another crime scene. Even then, that would only tell us the perps are committing a series of crimes, not who they are. Our best hope is that they'll pawn what they stole."

Shivering from a sudden gust, Ari backed into the cabin. "Very nice to meet you, Mal. I hope the robbers do try to pawn Sara's belongings so you can catch them."

"Nice meeting you too, ma'am. That's a beautiful bracelet."

"Isn't it?" She lifted her arm, the jewels sparkling in the wan light. "Harrison totally surprised me." She kissed me on the cheek and dashed deeper into the house.

I grabbed the door to close it, but the Ox, instead of walking away, stepped closer. "Sir, I'm assuming that's a very expensive piece of jewelry."

I stiffened. "I wouldn't give my wife paste."

"I'm sure of that. It's just that I've heard from a couple people that it's worth $20,000. If the price is that well known in the county — well, it could attract burglars."

A tide of hope welled within, but I put on a look of concern. "Do you think someone might try to break in here again?"

"It's possible. That bracelet gives them a definite reason."

Stroking my chin, I said, "I know how to set the alarm system properly now. That should deter any thief."

"Maybe. But I'll have my patrols hang around this area if they aren't on a call."

Perfect. One would think the Ox was my accomplice. I forced a broad smile. "Thank you, sheriff. You're very kind to strangers."

He stepped off the porch. "That's my job."

I shut the door as Ari hung up the phone. "Walter said he'll be here in an hour, and he'll build the fire for us." She skipped to me and kissed my nose. "Nothing is more romantic than a fire on a cold winter day."

~~~~~

Over an hour later, Walter the Woodcutter still had not arrived.

Shrugging on my coat, I told Ari I was going for a walk since the rain had seen fit to honor us with a break.

Ensconced in several fleeces on the repaired couch, she opened one of my novels. "I don't know how you can go out in this weather."

I expected that remark, which was why I didn't announce my intention until she was thoroughly comfortable.

She said, "You wouldn't go out in weather like this in New York unless you had to."

"Just one more change in me." I zipped my coat. "Is that novel your favorite?"

A pleased, Persian cat smile played over her coral lips. "All of
~~~~~

your books are my favorites."

Of course, they were. They had to be. They were the only fiction she had read since high school.

Leaving by the back door, I strode to the small outbuilding behind the house. I grabbed the shovel and walked as fast as I dared down the slope to the creek.

Prying the log off the buried goods, I glanced back up the hill. That Ari would leave her cocoon of comfort for the wilds of Sara's acreage was beyond far-fetched, but I had to maintain my guard.

I unearthed the garbage bag, untied the plastic straps closing it, and dug through its interior until I liberated the pair of tennis shoes, every exterior surface coated in mud.

Why hadn't I thought of this before? If I wanted to create the illusion that some local thug had heard about the bracelet and broken in to steal it, it made sense for him to be one of the robbers from the first break-in.

For a brilliant man, I had shocking lapses in intelligence.

I reburied the bag and shifted the log over it. Returning to the outbuilding, I leaned the shovel against the back wall and hid the shoes behind a stack of plastic pots.

Closing the door behind me, I noticed mud spattering my jeans and hands.

A mammoth truck, bearing more rust than paint, heaved up the driveway.

Walter the Woodcutter, most likely.

I descended the hill to the truck.

An imposing, elderly man emerged from the driver's side while a young woman, probably a teenager, as tall as me, exited the cab through the opposite door.

More bovines, which was understandable given their environment and breeding. But why did so many of them tend toward gigantism? The old man, walking stiffly, presented the dimensions of a bull abusing growth hormones.

"We got your wood." The old man owned a deep, craggy voice.

No introductions. Fine. I would adopt local custom. "This way." I took the steps up to the front porch.

The man and the girl, who seemed to consist of mostly gangly arms and legs, lifted several bundles of split wood from the bed of their truck. The old man climbed the stone steps, but the girl, for unknown reasons, started to hike up the slick slope.

She slipped and fell, of course, dropping her bundles, one of which burst its strapping, the thin logs tumbling down the small hill.

"Oh, you poor thing." Pulling on her lavender parka, Ari stepped onto the porch. "Are you all right?"

"Yes, ma'am." The girl achieved her feet, reddening, as she should, for making such a blunder. "Would you mind if I used your bathroom to clean up a little?" She held up mud-stained hands.

"Of course not," said Ari.

As the girl reached the porch without further difficulty, I said, "Take off your boots. If you track anything in, you're cleaning it up."

"Yes, sir." She untied a boot.

Ari rolled her eyes, very unattractive. "Give the girl a break, Harrison." She studied me a moment. "Did you fall on your walk?"

I wasn't anywhere near as muddy as that clumsy girl. "No. I saw a hole under Amy's outbuilding and filled it in."

Ari's mouth fell open, even more unattractive. "You helped someone?" She broke into a bewildered smile. "You have changed." She went inside with the girl.

"Rae's a good kid," said the old man, his deep-set eyes watching me without a shred of manners. "If she makes a mess, she'll clean it up."

Now that he stood beside me, the old man appeared even more bovine than the sheriff, his every feature massive and heavy. Only a nose ring was missing.

He clomped behind me to the fireplace.

After freeing the logs from their bindings, he knelt by the hearth. "I got a box in my truck with newspaper and kindling. Go get it."

I drew back as if I detected a stench. Who did this human bull think he was? "You were hired to bring wood and start a fire. If you can't do that, you won't be paid."

He eyed me from his crouched position. "You too fine to get a box?"

I arched an eyebrow. "I work with my brains, not my body, an activity I am sure is alien to you."

His gaze was oddly steady. "You can't work with your brains to find a box in my cab?"

Refusing to rise to the bait of this beast, I said, "Are you trying to give away this wood? That seems to be your intention."

"I brung it." He clambered to his feet. "You'll pay me."

My scorching glare pursued him to the door.

The old man returned surprisingly quickly with the box and the wood the girl had dropped. He had to be at least seventy-five.

I looked down the short, dark hall that led to the bedrooms and second bathroom. What was taking so long? Had the girl seriously injured herself and Ari was attempting amateur surgery?

As if by alchemy, the old man had a blaze burning in the grate. "You gotta keep feeding it. Use the kindling and smaller logs when it dies down. Don't put on the big ones until you get a steady burn."

"Thank you, Smokey the Bear." I went to the kitchen counter and retrieved my wallet.

He stood. "Twenty-five dollars."

I removed the bills and held them out to him. As his thick, calloused hand reached for them, I parted my fingers, and the bills drifted to the hardwood floor. "There's your—"

He sprang on me, clutching my throat and slamming me against the stone fireplace.

The pressure—the pressure …

Gasping, I grabbed at his hand.

Shoving his face to within an inch of mine, he said, his breath acrid, "I ain't some little girl you can make feel small."

I clawed his hand, but the motion had no effect on his grasp.

I was dying, dying right here, right here—

The old man leaned back, snatching my wallet from my hand and hurling me onto the hearth.

Groping for air, I righted myself into a seated position.

As he extracted two bills from my wallet, Ari and the girl walked into the living room.

"Harrison?" Ari rushed to my side. "What happened?"

Holding my throat, I struggled to my feet. "He tried to kill me." My voice was little more than a rasp.

The old man leered, revealing gray teeth. "You got a witness to back you up?"

"We can go, Walter," said the girl, her brown eyes wide,

edging toward the front door.

I stumbled up the three steps to the kitchen. "I'm calling the police."

"They know where to find me," he said without any concern. He stomped out the door, the girl trailing after him.

"You can't steal my wallet." I tried to shout, but it amounted to only a harsh whisper.

The old man returned to the doorway, filling it. "Fetch." He threw my wallet into the hall and stalked out of sight.

Blood flooded into my face. I snatched up the receiver.

Ari picked up my wallet. "I can't believe he—" Her delicate eyebrows jumping, she bent over and collected the money on the floor. "Oh, Harrison." She groaned. "I've told you. You'll fling your money down in front of the wrong person. I guess Walter was that person."

My grip driving the receiver into the flesh of my palm, I spun away from her. I hated that tone, hated that expression on her beautiful, infuriating face, hated that she had the nerve to file for divorce, advertising to the whole world what she thought of me.

I replaced the receiver in the holder. I had to focus on why I'd subjected myself to this descent into degradation.

"Are you hurt?" Ari walked up the steps to me.

"About time you cared." I released a long breath, resuming the act. "I don't have the time to come back here for a trial."

And I didn't want to attract the attention of the police until I was ready for them.

"Are you serious?" Again, the fish-like gawking. "You don't want to make him pay?"

"Only one thing will make me feel better." I pulled her close.

~~~~~

"I'm back when I said I'd be." Ariella bustled into the house late the next morning. "I guess I'm changing too. I got up early this morning and arrived somewhere on time." She offered me a cup of coffee.

"Why did you go into town?" Setting aside my briefcase, I took a tiny sip and made a face. The single compliment I could pay the beverage was that it was hot. "Your note only stated the time you'd be back."

"I just wanted to get out before you took the car for your
~~~~~

research trip." She pulled off her gloves. "Do you still think you can get enough material so we can leave by Wednesday?"

"Of course. I just booked a flight for that day." I brushed her cheek with my lips. "Thank you for the coffee. I don't know when I'll be back tonight. I may be late."

She returned the kiss. "I'll just relax. When I first came here, I thought I wouldn't be able to live without reception for my phone. But it's been so relaxing to disconnect. And reconnect with you."

We kissed again, an appropriate good-bye kiss. I collected my suitcase and coat.

As I drove away, Ari waved from the porch, her light brown hair straying across her face, her expression that combination of sultry and sweet that had graced so many magazine covers.

She looked content. Which was a good feeling to have on the last day of one's existence.

~~~~

I threw myself into the role of writer dedicated to his research, on the unlikely chance the police checked my whereabouts. While taking photos of plaques for Dawn Powell and John Crow Ransom and *The Kenyon Review*, I exchanged a few comments with anyone passing by. I endured tours at Malabar Farm State Park and Oak Hill Cottage, engaging the guides in lengthy conversations after explaining my intention to write an article on the Ohio Literary Trail. Stopping for supper in an insignificant town called Mt. Vernon, I lingered over my meal until it was truly dark.

In the rental, I dialed the cabin's landline. "Hello, lover. Just about to head home. It should only take me a couple of hours."

"I may not be up when you get here." Ari sounded tired. "I'm afraid I have a migraine starting."

"Then take your medicine and go to bed. I won't disturb you. Love you."

"Love you, too."

If she was in bed, my job would be much easier.

After two hours of driving through precipitation that changed from rain to snow on whims, I pulled over at the intersection of the state route and the road to the cabin. I changed my loafers for the tennis shoes and pulled on a ski mask, heavy gloves, and my coat. No matter how Ari struggled, she wouldn't leave a mark on me.

Using the flashlight from the house sparingly, I worked my
~~~~

way through the drenched, infernal woods, low branches slapping against my pants.

The cabin peeped through the trees, a light in the window of the living room the only visible illumination. I made a wide circle around the hovel, the damp seeping through the ill-made soles of my shoes. The rest of the house was dark.

Slipping off my mask, I walked to the back door, unlocked it, entered, and lifted the shield to the control panel for the alarm.

Strange. The warning beep hadn't blared to life.

I peered at the control screen. It indicated Ari hadn't bothered to set the alarm.

Very thoughtful.

Lowering the shield, I waited for Ari to greet me.

But the house was still, the hum of the refrigerator the only noise.

She must have gone to bed.

The light from a single lamp in the living room touched the kitchen. I found the drawer for utensils and withdrew the chef's knife. Tugging my mask into place, I passed through the living room and into the hall, my heart gathering speed.

The door to the master bedroom stood half open.

I pushed it aside and slipped into the room.

"Ari," I called softly to a mound of comforters and quilts on the queen-sized bed.

No sound, no movement.

"Ari."

No response.

I clenched the knife and my teeth. Had she taken a sedative instead of her migraine medicine? Her insensibility would drain all the enjoyment from my plan. She *had* to know she couldn't humiliate me in front of the whole world and steal my money. She *had* to know before she died.

I rounded the chest situated at the foot of the bed.

Silence.

As my heart rocketed into high velocity, I switched on the flashlight.

The mound was so high that I couldn't detect Ari's head. The bracelet twinkled on the nightstand. I'd pocket that when I was finished.

My grip tightening on the knife, my tongue running over my lips, I grabbed the hem of the comforter with the hand holding the light and jerked it off her.

"Ari!" I shouted.

But instead of revealing my dear wife, I found more blankets. And no sign of human reaction.

What was going on?

I whipped back the next cover, discovering a row of pillows arranged in human form.

A roar erupting through my teeth, I plunged back into the hall.

She couldn't have figured out my plan. Where was she?

"Police!" The nerve-shattering shout spun me into a blinding light.

"Drop the knife! Drop the knife!"

But how — but who — but — but —

The light vanished with a thunderous crash.

~~~~~

"It's all right, Mrs. Sharpe." Petite Deputy Lang touched my arm in the pitch blackness of the second bedroom. "That wasn't a shot. It sounded like something, or somebody, fell."

"Oh. Okay." Hugging myself, I took a breath, and the air scratched my throat.

From the hall outside came voices and people stepping and shuffling around.

Finally, the powerful voice of the sheriff went right through the closed door of the bedroom. "Mrs. Sharpe, would you please come out here?"

Deputy Lang opened the door.

In the hall, Sheriff Malinowski and the young deputy with the striking good looks named Kincaid crouched beside Harrison, who laid stretched out on the polished floor. Blood oozed from a cut on his temple.

Deputy Kincaid patted Harrison's cheeks. "Mr. Sharpe? Mr. Sharpe?"

The sheriff stood. "Mrs. Sharpe, does your husband have a medical condition that would cause him to suddenly lose consciousness?"

"No." Pulling my sweater closer around me, I said, "What happened? How did he hurt his head?"
~~~~~

Scratching his eyebrow, the sheriff said, "I think he fainted when I jumped out and told him to drop his weapon. He cracked his head on that little table before I could catch him. Call an ambulance, Kincaid."

A big kitchen knife shone in the light from the ceiling lamp.

Gulping, I clutched myself tighter. "Was Harrison carrying that knife?" My throat felt like someone had aimed a blowtorch down it.

"Ma'am, you look like you need to sit down." The sheriff motioned toward the living room. "Can I get you something to drink?"

"There's sparkling water in the refrigerator."

Holding onto the walls, I made it to the couch and perched on the edge. The sheriff handed me a tumbler of the water.

The long, cool sip soothed my burning throat. Although it was rotten posture, I sat hunched around my drink.

"I'm very sorry, Mrs. Sharpe." The sheriff took a seat on an easy chair.

I squinted at him. "Because you were right? You would have looked ridiculous if you'd been wrong."

"Ma'am, I would love looking ridiculous if I'd proved a husband actually wanted to reconcile with his wife."

Another sip, and my throat didn't feel torched anymore. I rolled back my shoulders and lengthened my spine, focusing on the sheriff's midnight blue eyes like I did when I gave an interview. "Would you please go over again how you figured out what Harrison was up to? When you tried to explain things at the coffee shop this morning, I didn't understand it all. I guess I was too shocked. And I didn't really believe you."

"That's understandable. I'm glad you agreed to this trap, anyway."

I sipped again. "I had to know if I really had a chance to salvage our marriage." The last two words caught on my tongue, and I set the tumbler on the end table. "You said something about the robbery made you suspicious. The guns, I think."

"Yes, ma'am." He pulled a pad from his overloaded belt. "They didn't fit. They were the kind of small, valuable items the thieves would go for. So they would take them off the hooks, feel how light they were, and realize they were fakes. What would they do next? Well, they'd committed a lot of senseless vandalism as they went through the house, so the most likely thing for them to do was throw the guns on the floor. Thieves who had ripped open cushions and broken furniture wouldn't replace the guns carefully on their hooks."

Glancing at the pad, he said, "The next morning, I called Ms. Novak to ask her if she could come up with a list of things that might have been stolen. I also asked about Mr. Sharpe—what kind of person he was. She told me how stunned she was Mr. Sharpe wanted to rent her cabin. He'd always talked about how he hated the country. And she mentioned that he was in the middle of a difficult divorce.

"So I had a few suspicions. Then my older sister gave me another one when she met your husband at the National Road Museum."

I said, "Was that one of those literary places Harrison was researching?"

He nodded. "Supposed to be researching. My sister Jeanine's a writer—mysteries. She saw your husband walk into the museum, which has an exhibit about an author named Zane Grey. But instead of talking to the staff, Mr. Sharpe just took a few pictures and left after ten minutes. When Jeanine stopped and asked him if he needed help, he said his readers wouldn't be interested in a writer of westerns. Couldn't he have decided that from an internet search?

"I contacted Ms. Novak again and asked if she could find out who he was writing his article for. By the way, Ms. Novak seems to've been waiting her whole life to dish the dirt on Harrison Sharpe."

My laugh came out as a kind of huff. "The entire New York literary community has."

"When she got back with me, Ms. Novak said none of the editors she knew Mr. Sharpe usually writes for had heard of an article on the Ohio Literary Trail." He flipped a page on his pad. "That could still mean he was writing for someone she didn't know of, but she assured me that your husband would only write for a very prestigious publication or one with a huge reader base.

"Then I heard about what happened to Claire and that you had joined your husband, and he had given you an expensive bracelet.

And I got very worried."

"Who is—oh, Claire." I pushed my hand over the top of my hair. "She was our waitress at the lodge. Harrison was obnoxious to her, but why did that worry you?"

"While you were in the bathroom, he threw her tip on the floor."

My hand falling limp, I groaned. "He couldn't leave her alone, so he got me out of the way."

"Yes, ma'am. That's what set off my alarm bells. If your husband was determined to get revenge on a waitress for an accident, what would he do to his wife for divorcing him? And then suddenly, it made sense why he was staying in a place he loathed."

"Why? I agree with Sara. This was the last place I thought Harrison would want to write about."

He smiled with one side of his mouth. "Mr. Sharpe thought it'd be a whole lot easier to trick a bunch of hillbilly cops than New York's finest into thinking your murder was just a robbery gone wrong." He shook his head and then said, "Since I couldn't call you, I came here yesterday, hoping to find you alone, so I could tell you my suspicions. And that's all I had. No evidence at all."

A knock from the front door made me jump, and Mal got up and let the paramedics in, telling them where to find Harrison.

Sitting again in the easy chair, he said, "Unfortunately, your husband was here. I went through the charade of asking him to go over his story again as I tried to figure out a way to contact you. Then you asked about buying firewood, and your husband said he had the number of somebody named Walter. I knew right then I had a way to deliver a message to you."

Putting my head to one side, I said, "Is there only one Walter around here?"

He rolled his eyes to the ceiling. "Yes, and believe me, he's enough. I left here as soon as I could without arousing your husband's suspicions and got a hold of Walter. Then I asked my daughter if she would go with him to deliver my message—you were in danger and if you could get away from your husband to call me, I'd meet you anywhere."

I grabbed the tumbler and took a long drink. The facts were piling up too fast. "So that nice girl really was your daughter? Not a deputy?"

His face lit up like a photographer had turned a studio light on it. "Yes, that's Rae. I couldn't risk a deputy. If your husband had picked Marlin County as the scene of his crime because he thought law enforcement here was incompetent, I couldn't be sure how much research he'd done on my personnel. A female would find it easier to talk to you alone. Rae's extremely smart. I knew she could pull it off. But when she came home, she was convinced you didn't believe her."

"I didn't at first. I thought it was some kind of weird joke because Harrison had been so difficult with people here. But then—" I frowned at my clasped hands. "I couldn't get what she said out of my mind. Harrison seemed to have changed, but at other times, he acted like the same selfish, nasty jerk he's always been. Like with the waitress. And with Walter." I looked up. "Did Walter tell you that Harrison threw his money on the floor?"

"Oh, yeah." Mal put a ton of feeling behind those two words. "Your husband should be grateful he only needs an ambulance for a crack on the head. Friday night, I heard about what happened to Claire and got over to Walter's place just before he and a gang of our male relatives, along with some female ones who enjoy a good beating, left to explain to Mr. Sharpe how they didn't care for his treatment of Claire."

I stared. "Why should Walter be angry about what—" My eyes flew open. "Did you say 'our male relatives'?"

"Walter's my grandfather. Claire's too. She's one of my cousins—one of my many, many cousins. I knew it was risky sending Walter with the firewood when he wanted to separate your husband from this life, but it was the only way I knew I could contact you safely. I explained to Walter that your husband was under investigation and I needed him to remain in the condition Walter found him. He almost complied."

I couldn't stop staring. "Is everybody in this county related to you?"

He chuckled. "I have my suspicions."

"What do you think you're doing?" Harrison's voice rang loud and clear from the hall.

Slumping back on the couch, I was too tired to pay attention anymore, but I had to ask, "So now you have your evidence?"

Mal got to his feet. "Your husband will have a hard time

explaining away how he acted here tonight, but I'm sure he'll try."
He told me what Harrison did after he came into the cabin.

My breathing reducing to spurts, I held my head in my hands.

"Mrs. Sharpe, why don't you spend the rest of your time here
with my sister? She can put you up."

I lifted my face. Cops were supposed to be helpful. I hadn't
expected them to be kind. "Thank you. And you're right. Harrison
will try to talk his way out of this."

"But he can't talk his way out of physical evidence. And I'm
sure your husband has provided me with that after the hint I
dropped yesterday." He slipped his pad into a holder on his belt.
"Mr. Sharpe is an intelligent man. If he thought the big, dumb
sheriff needed a certain kind of proof to believe you were killed by
ordinary thieves, he'd break his neck to furnish it." He moved to
the hall. "I'll see if Kincaid and Lang have collected it."

~~~~~

It was ridiculous to handcuff me to this stretcher. As if I would
escape when my head felt like it had been cleaved in two.

The cow acting as a paramedic finished bandaging my head,
and I laid back, shutting my eyes.

The Ox had nothing on me.

So what that the police would find my car at the intersection?
I slid off the road and had to walk to the cabin.

I wore a ski mask. The weather was freezing.

I carried a knife. Through the window, I saw the silhouette of
a man inside the house and entered by the back door to get a
weapon. When Ari didn't come or call to me, I hurried to our
bedroom, sick with worry, and became even sicker when I couldn't
find her in our bed.

I smiled, but that slight motion shot pain up to my injured
temple.

Everything I'd done could be assigned an innocent
explanation.

The second cow grabbed the front of the stretcher and jerked
me toward the living room, making my head throb.

The Ox stepped into the hall. "Just a minute."

"As soon as I can get to a phone," I lifted myself as best I could
on my elbows, "I'm telling my lawyer to bring a charge of police
brutality."
~~~~~

That should have given him food for thought while daring to arrest me.

Without acknowledging I'd spoken, he lifted the blanket from my feet.

My headache soaring to mind-splitting, I gouged the cold metal of the railings into my hands.

He untied and removed both tennis shoes. Then he straightened, his gaze stabbing mine, the left side of his mouth rising.

Shrinking back to the pillow, I crumpled the blanket against my chest.

Why now, out of an utter vacuum, didn't he look in the least bovine?

END

To read more about Rae and Sheriff Malinowski, check out the short story "A Rose from the Ashes" in *Christmas fiction off the beaten path* and the novel *A Shadow on the Snow*.

Ohio Literary Trail Sites in "Bovine":

John Crow Ransom and The Kenyon Review in Gambier, Ohio
This plaque in Knox County memorializes one of the most distinguished literary magazines in America.

Dawn Powell in Mt. Gilead, Ohio
This plaque in Morrow County memorializes the birthplace of a novelist and playwright.

Oak Hill Cottage in Mansfield, Ohio
This house is an example of Gothic Revival architecture and is an important setting in Louis Bromfield's novel, "The Green Bay Tree." Tours are available, Visit oakhillcottage.org.

Malabar Farm State Park in Pleasant Valley in Richland County
Best-selling novelist Louis Bromfield moved back to Ohio in the 1930s with his family after years of living in France. He built a mansion

onto the farmhouse that came with the property and promoted agricultural practices that were environmentally friendly. You can tour the house and the property. Since it's a state park, there are hiking trails and campsites. A fun day trip. Learn more at ohiodnr.gov and malabarfarm.org.

Fun fact: My great-grandparents lived on a farm near Mr. Bromfield and my dad remembers visiting him at Malabar Farm with his grandparents when he was a child in the 1950s.

National Road and Zane Grey Museum in Norwich Ohio

This museum in Muskingum County has a recreation of the study of novelist Zane Grey, who was born in Zanesville, Ohio. Although he wrote in several genres, he is best remembered for his Westerns. Visitors will also see a huge diorama chronicling the history and importance of the National Road and a beautiful display about local pottery. The staff were very friendly and knowledgeable. Another lovely day trip. To learn more, visit ohiohistory.org.

Thurber House Museum and Thurber Center in Columbus

Writer and humorist James Thurber lived in this house with his family while attending Ohio State University. It is now a literary arts center. To learn more, visit thethurberhouse.org.

JPC Allen started her writing career in second grade with an homage to Scooby Doo. She's been tracking down mysteries ever since. Her Christmas mystery, A Rose from the Ashes, was a Selah-finalist at the Blue Ridge Mountains Christian Writers Conference in 2020. Her first novel, a YA mystery, A Shadow on the Snow, released in 2021. Online, she offers tips and prompts to ignite the creative spark in every kind of writer. Coming from a long line of Mountaineers, she is a life-long Buckeye. Follow her to her next mystery at JPCAllenWrites.com and on Facebook and Instagram @JPCAllenWrites.

BETWEEN SEMICOLONS AND PLOT TWISTERS
by Rebecca Waters

"No!" The young woman screamed. Tears flowed down her face as the burly man grabbed her arm and slapped her. The stench of sweat and the roughness of his hands sickened her "Please let me go," she begged. "Please!"

The man wrestled her arms behind her, stumbling slightly as she twisted and turned, crying all the while. "Shut up!" he snarled. He tightened his grip. The last words she heard before the sweaty palm jerked her head aside were, "You're worthless!"

With those words all light died. So did her spirit.

Chapter 1

Mount Adams, Cincinnati, Ohio
Winter

Beth Michael stared at the screen on her laptop.

"How's your new book coming, baby?"

Beth smiled at her husband of eleven years. "Actually, I was reading this email from my writing club."

"Which club?" John rummaged through the refrigerator. "Say, are we out of creamer?"

"Bottom shelf in the door. Actually it's from Scott in the Plot Twisters. He sent a list of writers who have some connection with Ohio. He wants us to identify one we'd like to know more about and share a quick bio of that person with the club at our next meeting."

"Could be interesting."

Beth frowned. "Sounds like homework to me."

John handed Beth her cup of coffee and sat down at the kitchen table near her. "But I know you, sweetheart, you'll do it. You're a pleaser."

"I don't like it when you say that."

"You may not like it but it's true. Then again, that's why you did so well in school, right?"

"I guess. These authors are all over the state. James Thurber, Erma Bombeck. I always liked her sense of humor. You should see this list. Sharon Draper. Did I ever tell you I met her once?"

"Maybe. Let me see the screen."

Beth turned her laptop so they could both view the list as she scrolled through. "Some of these people I'm not all that familiar with…you?"

"As an English professor, I should be, perhaps, but no. Look at these." John pointed to the screen. "I knew Zane Grey was from Ohio, but I never knew Sue Grafton had an Ohio connection."

"Me neither." The two continued sifting through the long list of authors. "Here's one I really should know, but in truth know very little about… Harriet Beecher Stowe. And she's listed as having a Cincinnati connection. I think I'll claim her to research before someone else does."

"Where did Scott get this list?"

Beth returned to the original email. "He doesn't say. Just that he wants us to be thinking about it and research one of the authors on the list for next month's meeting."

"Will you have time? I mean with the last book in the series and all. I know you said you were struggling to make it happen."

"The problem, John, is my heart isn't into writing these sweet little cozy mysteries anymore."

"I thought you liked that whole gig."

Beth leaned back in the chair. "When I started writing, it was fun. I thought I was offering something entertaining that wasn't evil and dark. Writing made it possible for me to be a stay-at-home mom. It seemed like something God wanted me to do. And, I admit, I liked getting published. Now, it all seems frivolous. Lately, I've been thinking I want to write something that makes a difference in people's lives."

John took another sip of coffee, stood, and kissed his wife's forehead. "You do make a difference. Every day. At least in our lives. But if you're having second thoughts, why don't you take some time off? Pray about it and maybe talk to Angie."

The image of the energetic agent brought a smile. At twenty-nine, Angela Parks was making a name for herself in the Christian writing market as a go-getter. Beth was the first to sign with Angie seven years ago when they were both breaking into the writing industry. Now Beth proved to be one of Angie's most successful and prolific writers.

"Time off? Maybe after I finish the last book in the River Valley series. I think I'll wait to say anything to Angie."

But pray? Yes, God. I need desperately to talk with You about what's next.

John threw his jacket on and headed toward the door. "It'll all come together. Bye, babe!"

The idea of having a regular workday with a lunch hour chatting with fellow professors and students sounded amazing and simple to Beth. As head of the English department at the university, John taught the classes he wanted and was able to choose his own schedule. Of course, there were other duties but when he was home he managed to leave work behind. *And he's changing lives, God.*

Beth looked at the clock. One hour before she needed to wake up Lily and Violet, get them dressed, fed, and out the door to catch the bus for school. With luck, Iris would sleep in a bit. One hour. *Write or pray?*

"Both." Beth pecked at the keyboard, compiling a prayer list. "My family of course. Direction in my writing. Meera." Beth looked up from the screen. "Meera." She allowed herself to travel the more than 8,000 miles to India, reliving the ten days she spent there a year before Iris was born. "Is that the direction I need to take for my writing, Lord? But how? How can I write such a story? How would it make Meera feel?" *Would she ever know?*

Before she could consider the idea more, a loud crash came from upstairs, followed by crying. Beth dashed up the stairs to Iris's nursery. There, in the middle of the floor sat Lily holding Iris, rocking her back and forth and whispering calming words over her little sister.

"I think she wanted out of her crib, Mom."

Beth reached for her youngest child. "*How* did she get out of her crib? Did you help her?"

Lily shrugged. "I don't know how she got out."

Violet came in from the bathroom holding a wet washcloth, "Me, either, Mommy."

"Thank you, girls. Now get ready for school. I'll take care of your sister." Beth wiped Iris's tear-stained face and bounced her on her hip. "You're becoming a little escape artist, aren't you? I think we're going to have to put that crib away."

Iris stuck her thumb in her mouth and laid her head on her mother's shoulder. Beth stroked the child's back as they made their way down the stairs.

"I wasn't getting much done, anyway. My heart just isn't into this book." Beth patted her daughter on the back. *There's a story in my heart, but this one isn't it.* "Maybe you and I should make pancakes for breakfast for your sisters. What do you say?"

Chapter 2

Walnut Hills, Cincinnati, Ohio
Winter

Harriet untied the bonnet and gently removed it from her hair pinned beneath it, while Calvin lit the lamp. "I'll see to the children," he told her.

Harriet watched as Calvin slipped up the kitchen staircase. She stoked the fire in the iron stove and set the pot of water on to boil. "All snug?" she asked as her husband returned.

"Every last one fast asleep." Calvin set the cups on the table.

"Your commentary on the current state of education and the need for uniformity in teacher training, dear husband, was well received. I think you shall have no difficulty finding a suitable publisher. All members of the Semicolon group deemed it ready."

"It is one thing to impress members of our writing group and quite another to capture the imagination of Ohio's governing officials. They are my real audience."

"I trust they will listen," she said.

"Was the good Dr. Drake quizzing you again about your experience with hydrotherapy? I only ask because I saw you shake your head with a rather emphatic *no*."

"It wasn't that. He was responding to my comment about wanting to write something of value. Perhaps something that would make a difference in the lives of others. He suggested I write about the treatment, as it is becoming a rather accepted practice for a number of illnesses. I explained it is much too personal for me to write about yet. It was not an unpleasant conversation. Unlike that I had with James Hall."

"James? Pray tell, what did the man say?" Calvin said.

"He wants me to write more character sketches akin to those I supplied him of the New England folk. I suggested something from the territories or even here on the western front, but he seeks to portray the more genteel way of life of the East."

"I understand. But, my dear, his *Western Monthly Magazine* has a broad audience and your New England Sketches were well received. I see his point."

"I would like to write something for the cause, if anything, but of course as you know, I am preparing another work for the *New York Evangelist*. I told James as much. Please, let's not speak more of James just now. I hold the man in high regard despite what I see as his desire to shape Cincinnati into another Philadelphia."

Calvin sipped his tea and put his cup down. "Very well. Caroline's new novel sounds interesting."

"Indeed. I find myself caught betwixt and between. I enjoy the art of storytelling through the printed text as does Caroline, all the while desirous of teaching the simple truths of the Holy Scripture and of course, the cause."

"My dear wife, you write more than any of us. You say you are betwixt and between, yet your stories always have a valuable moral lesson or at the very least they are exemplary of the model of decorum expected in most social circles. And your studies on the scripture are written in such a way the ordinary person can fully grasp the deeper meaning and import of the Bible text. I believe, Harriet, that is because you understand the power of the story better than I."

"You flatter me, Mr. Stowe."

"Flatter? You consider my comments insincere? I speak these as simple truths, not flattery. Were my own expositions as easily grasped as are yours, I would be an extremely happy man. I would leave behind my work at the seminary to produce mountains of texts for seminary students and the lay person to devour at will."

Harriet smiled. "One day, perhaps that is what you will do."

"No. I am more likely to agent your work than my own."

A laugh escaped her. "That, I truly doubt."

"I am not being foolish, my dear wife." Calvin leaned in. "Trust me, Harriet. God has gifted you with talent and given you the tenacity to see it through. Many talk of writing or publishing. You do it. And you do not waste your time waiting to hear about one manuscript before creating another."

"I agree that much of what I have constructed has found its way into print, but much hasn't as well."

"It matters not what is published. What matters is that you continue to write. One day, sweet woman, you will find the time and place optimal to craft the story in your heart. The one you long to write."

Calvin's words echoed in Harriet's thoughts as she fell to sleep that night. *The story in my heart.*

Chapter 3

Mount Adams, Cincinnati, Ohio
Spring

"I'm sorry I'm late." Beth set her book bag on the table.

John walked into the kitchen. "No problem. The girls are in bed. I let Lily read another chapter in her book before lights out. That girl is turning into a reading machine." The two walked into the living room. "So how was your group?"

Beth sighed as she tossed her notebook on the end table. "Okay, I guess. They helped me with a major plot point I needed."

"That's why they call themselves the Plot Twisters."

"True. The problem is, I don't think they understand why I want to finish this series and leave the world of cozy mysteries behind for a while."

"Was Danielle there? She seems to support you."

"She was there. And yes, you're right, she supports my desire to write something meaningful. The others say I have a good gig going."

"Well, sweetheart, you have to remember you've published more than they have. You have three series under your belt and a contract for the fourth. Not to mention your first two standalone novels."

"I know. And I should be grateful. It's just that there is this story I feel I need to write, but I can't get a handle on it."

"I know. Ever since your mission trip to India you've talked about it. When the time is right, honey. When the time is right. Did you share your info on Harriet Beecher Stowe?"

"No. Not everyone had claimed an author or done the work, so Scott said we'll do it next time."

"Think of it as being ahead of the pack." With that, John sauntered into the family room and turned on the television. Soon the voice of one of Cincinnati's sportscasters filled the room.

Beth wandered upstairs, peeked in on her daughters, tucked snugly in their beds, and headed to the master suite she and John called their "retreat." She kicked off her shoes, started the bathwater and poured in a double dose of foaming bath salts.

As the tub filled, Beth walked to the bookshelf by the bed. She ran her fingers over the books she called her "game-changer" collection. Thirteen books that changed lives.

"*Diary of a Young Girl*, my first encounter with Anne Frank and the horrors of Nazi Germany. *I Am Malala*. Stories that open people's eyes." Beth drew her hand to her heart. "Stories of lives I would not want to have lived but books I wish I could write. Books that enlighten. Books that make a difference."

The fragrant bath relaxed muscles she didn't realize were tense. Ideas rolled around in her head as the water slowly cooled. Relaxed and ready for bed, Beth slipped between the cool sheets and under the light cover her grandmother had stitched together for her from colorful cotton feed sacks. A summer quilt, her grandmother called it.

A patchwork. Stitched together like life. Yet some lives, like quilts, aren't made of useful feed sacks. Some are stitched together from rags. It was the last thought she had before surrendering to a deep and restful sleep.

Chapter 4

Walnut Hills, Cincinnati, Ohio
Spring

Harriet stepped up onto the porch.

"Look, Mother," Eliza said as she thrust a paper up within an inch of Harriet's face. "Aunt Catharine said my story of the boy in the apple tree is excellent. And my penmanship is coming along nicely."

Harriet leaned back and gently nudged the paper away from her face an inch or so before taking it in hand. "Ah, yes, Eliza. Your penmanship is excellent. Is this the story you told me about? The one where the boy witnesses an infraction on Mrs. Williams' garden by those ruffian boys, but to report it must also mean he confesses he was in her apple tree stealing apples?"

"Yes, Mother. The other boys caused much more harm than did he, but he wishes not to tell anyone because of his own misdirection in the matter."

"And what did the boy decide?"

Eliza grinned and handed her mother the paper before skipping off. "If you want to see how it ends, you must read the story, Mother," she called over her shoulder.

Harriet laughed and entered the back door of the tall brick house. Her sister, Catharine, placed a stack of books on the shelf and picked up a slate from the floor.

"I long for those days of school," Harriet said, removing her bonnet and patting the pins in her hair in place. "Remember the debates we had in Hartford at the Female School? Sometimes when Calvin heads out the gate toward the seminary, I long to go after him, if only to engage in daily conversation with the intellects of the day."

"Intellect does not reside in the school, dear sister, but rather in the mind. Be it not enough stimulation to have me here to challenge your every word?"

Harriet laughed. "Dear sister of mine, where would I be, nay, where would any of us be without your care and devotion to me and to my family?"

Catharine reached out and touched Harriet lightly on the arm. "Your health is so much better now, Harriet. I should not be surprised if you objected to my role as teacher of my nieces and nephews at some point and took over the job yourself."

"And deny my own children the expertise of one of the most highly educated women in America?"

"We jest now, but soon Henry will be of an age where he will be going off to school and away from the musings of his aging aunt and..." Catharine let the end of her thoughts trail off as she dusted the chalk from her hands.

Harriet stiffened. "And what? His melancholy mother? Or perhaps you were thinking his severely depressed parent."

Catharine stared back at her younger sister. "Actually, I wasn't thinking of you at all. I was about to say he would be forming his own opinions on matters. But if I were to address the issue of you, my sister, I would certainly conjure up a word more worthy of your talent and drive. Tenacious, perhaps. Yet that only captures half of it, doesn't it?"

Harriet closed her eyes, her head bent down. "I beg your forgiveness, Catharine. You have done nothing but offer tender care both to me and to my family. Though I am quite well now, those many months away from my husband and children presses me from every side."

"It is the devil himself seeking to cause you harm, Harriet. It is not uncommon for a woman to falter after childbirth. Remember, too, our dear brother's death previous that time, and though you oppose my saying so, your own husband's devotion to the seminary has taken him from you when you needed him most."

"Do not blame Calvin for fulfilling his obligation to his work. His work is of the Lord's and puts food on the table. He must do all he can to recruit students and raise funds." Harriet picked up Georgie's pinafore from the back of the chair, folded it, and drew in a deep breath. "Is Georgie napping?"

"Yes, Hattie carried her upstairs a few minutes ago. I must get back to Father's house to prepare the evening meal now. Lydia is in New York for the month visiting her daughter."

Harriet smiled. "I think you do most of the cooking even when our dear stepmother is home, Catharine."

"It is a small offering. Lydia does much to help Father. He is happy enough with the arrangement. Though..."

"Though? Though what?"

Catharine paused as she donned her bonnet. "I long for New England. I'll remain in Cincinnati as long as I am needed, but one day I wish to return to Connecticut."

Harriet touched her sister's arm. "One day, perhaps, but for now I must state that without your assistance, Father's house may stand, but mine would surely fall apart."

Chapter 5

Mount Adams, Cincinnati, Ohio
Summer

"Hey, Sweetie! How'd it go?" John turned off the television.

Beth tossed her book bag on the sofa. "Pretty good. We didn't get very far though with our critiques. We spent the first hour talking about field trips."

"Field trips? What kind of field trips?"

Beth plopped down on the sofa next to her book bag. "Ever hear of something called the Ohio Literary Trail?"

"Sure. One of the professors at the university sat in on some of the Ohioana meetings. They're the real force behind it. I haven't seen the map, but it shows where authors either lived or worked in Ohio. I take it this has something to do with researching the Ohio authors."

"Exactly. Allison read about it in her Triple-A magazine and sent Scott the info. That's where he got the idea to have us research authors with a connection to Ohio. Anyway, the group decided we'll visit the sites we can, we'll each do some research on one of the featured authors, share that info with all of the Plot Twister members and arrange for a field trip for everyone."

John grinned and raised his brows. "Everyone?"

Beth looked up. "Yes, everyone. Families included. You interested?"

"I think it would be great for the girls." John moved to his desk and pulled up the Ohio Literary Trail on his laptop. "And I would enjoy some of it, too."

Beth joined him as he zoomed in on the map of the Cincinnati area. "This is good. The Harriet Beecher Stowe House in Walnut Hills is close."

"Some of these sites aren't actual tours you could take, though." John pointed at the list. "These are historical markers. They're likely a sign in the ground marking 'so-and-so was here.' But there are a few actual museums or libraries, see?"

The two studied the map. They took turns reading the descriptions. They read through each region on the map. "There are several around here. And..." John drew a large circle with his finger on the computer screen. "I think these are all doable for us to see as a family."

"Yes, but..." Beth's voice trailed off.

"You sound skeptical."

"Oh, sure, I know we can get those sites in, it's just that we've all been given the challenge to write a story including the person and the site."

"So you write up our visit."

"It's more than that. We agreed to write a short story for an anthology of stories taking place in Ohio by Ohio authors."

"Like your *From the Lake to the River* anthology?"

Beth stood. "Exactly. Except we have to weave the Ohio Literary Trail into the story and we have to include something about the author whose venue we visited."

"I don't see the problem."

"John, I write contemporary stuff. I don't see how I could weave a writer from the 1800s into a contemporary story."

"You'll figure it out and it'll be great."

"Maybe."

John closed his laptop, stood, and pulled Beth close. "When is this story due?"

"We haven't discussed the due date yet. Sometime early next year, I suppose."

"Good, then you have time to get your last series out, use this little story as a respite, and ready yourself to write that book you've been putting off."

Beth looked up at her husband's smiling face. "You are such an encourager. And you're right. This short story may be just the ticket to get my head out of the world of cozy mysteries."

Chapter 6

Walnut Hills, Cincinnati, Ohio
Summer, 1846

"Excuse me, Mother."

Harriet looked up from the blank paper in front of her. "This must be something quite important since you're being so polite, Henry."

"I wish to gain your permission to go to Thomas's house."

"I assume you've completed your chores."

"Yes, Mother. Thomas Allen invited me to play badminton."

Harriet grinned at her nearly eight-year-old son. "You may go, but you must promise to be home for supper."

"Yes, ma'am!" Henry darted toward the screen door. "Thank you, Mother!"

Harriet watched as Henry flew off the porch and down the hill. The image of William, a main character in one of her short stories, loomed large. "A boy, perhaps, but older than Henry." Harriet closed her eyes and imagined her son at eighteen. A smile crossed her face, but faded quickly as she picked up her pen and began working on her latest story, which she intended to call *The Coral Ring*.

"A simple story to both entertain and make known the cause for temperance," she'd told members of her writing group, the Semicolon Club. She frowned at the thought of Henry taking to intemperate habits.

The chiming of the hall clock an hour later beckoned her to abandon her writing and address the task of the evening meal. Harriet called to her ten-year-old twins to set aside the books they were reading to help set the table.

"It's a trick worth remembering," Harriet told her daughters, Hattie and Eliza. "Always set the table first. It makes the men feel as though the meal is nearly ready and they won't grumble."

"Then they only need complain about the food," Eliza offered.

"Well, I may not be as great a cook your Aunt Catharine, but I don't see your father or the boys withering away."

One girl folded the linen napkins and placed them by each plate while the other arranged the silver utensils according to what their Aunt Catharine assured them was a proper place setting.

"Where are Fredrick and Georgie?" Hattie asked. "At least Georgie should be helping us."

"Your brother is working on his letters and Georgie's likely dawdling or in the privy. She'll be along soon. I told your sister she could help me make biscuits," Harriet told them.

"But Mother, I always help make the biscuits," Eliza said.

"As do I," Hattie whined.

"Indeed. However, I think it is time you girls learned a new skill. The blackberries are ripe. I picked some this morning while the dew was still on them." Harriet turned to her oldest children, a twinkle in her eye. "Today the two of you shall prepare blackberry pie. Your father's favorite."

Harriet placed the last of the china on the table and the three headed toward the kitchen.

"Georgie!" all three cried out simultaneously.

The three-year-old wiped blackberry-stained hands on her pinafore and gave them all a broad berry-seeded smile. "I wike backberries!" she called out.

Harriet sighed and turned to the twins. "See what you can salvage. I'll see to your sister. I fear she needs a little cleaning up and a good talking to."

Chapter 7

Mount Adams, Cincinnati, Ohio
Late Summer

Beth stared intently at the image of the Harriet Beecher Stowe house filling her computer screen.

John leaned over and kissed his wife on the forehead. "How's your research on Harriet Beecher Stowe going?"

"Pretty good, actually. I'm learning a lot about the woman I never imagined. I knew she wrote *Uncle Tom's Cabin*, but John, she wrote so much more. She wrote articles for a publication called *Godey's Lady's Book*. It must have been a magazine for women. But she also wrote tons of articles on the Bible and on slavery. You know, not stories, more like essays. And she wrote short stories to teach moral truths. I guess *Uncle Tom's Cabin* was her most famous book, but even that started as a series of stories for a weekly newspaper."

"I don't think I actually ever read it, but I remember hearing one time a quote from Abraham Lincoln about it. Supposedly he met Mrs. Stowe and said something like, 'So this is the little lady who started this big war.'"

"I read about that encounter in my research. She was very short, not even five feet tall, and he was well over six feet. That would have been something to witness."

"It'll be interesting to go with your group to tour her house."

"Actually, the Stowe house we're visiting in Walnut Hills was her father's residence. She lived there for about three years before she married and moved a bit down the hill, but in the same area. Several of her children were born at her father's house, though. He was the president of the Lane Seminary. Ever hear of it?"

"Doesn't ring a bell."

"Apparently there was a big debate there over slavery and Harriet witnessed it."

"Wait a minute. Yes, the Lane Debates. I think they lasted for days. When I sat in on the planning committee for the Freedom Center, I remember that coming up."

"I need to visit the Freedom Center. It's been maybe ten years or more since I was there."

"What is it they say about 'things in your own back yard'?"

"It could be a good trip for us before we go to the Stowe House." Beth opened her day planner to scour the dates available.

"Us, meaning your writing group?"

"Actually, I was thinking about us as a family. Lily and Violet are old enough to appreciate some of it, I'm sure. We'll get a sitter for Iris. What do you think?"

"It's a good idea, though are you sure the girls are old enough?"

Beth turned her head to the picture of herself with her Indian friend, Meera, on the mantle. "Yes. Absolutely."

Chapter 8

Walnut Hills, Cincinnati, Ohio
Late Summer

Harriet shuddered, her eyes springing open.

"Mother?"

Harriet shook off the image of the woman crying as her child was taken from her arms. "What is it, Fredrick?" Harriet pulled herself straight in the overstuffed parlor chair.

"I didn't mean to disturb you, Mother, but I'm having some difficulty with my letters." The young boy handed his writing slate to his mother. "Henry says my 'S' looks like nothing but string."

Harriet smiled as she studied the slate filled with rows of the letter S. "Well, at least your string is standing rather tall as it should. I doubt Henry remembers his early writing was scrunched and all the letters landed in a heap. Try another row and circle the best ones for me." Harriet watched as her son headed toward the kitchen table.

"I seem a bit tired these days," Harriet admitted to Catharine the following day. "Even yesterday, I sat down for the span of five minutes and in that short amount of time I drifted into a dream of sorts. It was another era, but I wasn't there long enough to make sense of it."

"You work too hard, sister. You need manage six children, most under the age of ten. You have a garden to tend, meals to put on the table, and of course there is your compulsion to write. Not to mention your charity work and the volunteer work you do for the church and Lane Seminary. I don't see how any woman would not be tired in the afternoon."

"Perhaps you're right. At the Brattleboro Institute, the message was always about finding balance. Not merely balance of the body's humors, but in all areas of life as well. I shall keep a diary as I did during my hydrotherapy sessions. Perhaps I will learn the reason for my fatigue.

~~~~~

The dream started the same as always, but this night, as the shadows fell across the quilt her own mother stitched, Harriet yielded to the story unfolding in her mind's eye. She could hear the clip-clopping of horse hooves on the cobblestone road as the buggy made its way into the small Kentucky town.

Harriet knew her host, Marshall Key and her father did not see eye-to-eye on all matters, but Mr. Key was a supporter of the Seminary and sent his daughter to study there. It was his daughter, Elizabeth, who requested Harriet join her for a stay at her home in Washington, Kentucky, for a few days that summer.

Elizabeth greeted Harriet at the door and welcomed her into the large hall. A young woman with skin the hue of creamy coffee served them biscuits and tea. The dream seemed to jump
~~~~~

immediately to the bedroom Harriet occupied during her stay.

Harriet allowed the soft feather bed to swallow her like the warm hug of her mother, now gone more than forty years. Morning sun poured in from the window. Harriet woke to the sounds of horses and carriages below. For a moment, she was yet in the Key house until the fog of sleep ebbed slowly away and the odd shapes turned in her mind to the furnishings in her own bedroom in Cincinnati. She let her fingers trace the intricate appliques on the quilt left to her by her mother, Roxana.

I awoke this morning thinking I was once again in the Marshall Key house in Kentucky, she wrote a short time later. *It is a dream often repeated but never finished. Perhaps this business of unfinished dreams is causing my fatigue. I shall continue to write these experiences down in the hope of finding the answer. Yet, I fear the dream. Shall hope again win over fear or will I succumb to the fear forever?* Harriet leaned back from the desk in her bedroom and closed the inkwell. "Perhaps it is the dream alone I fear," she spoke into the empty room. "A troubling dream."

Chapter 9

Mount Adams, Cincinnati, Ohio
Autumn

Beth closed her Bible and pulled the picture from the pocket of the Bible cover. The big, brown eyes of the young girl drew her into another time. "Meera," she whispered. Beth touched the picture lightly and prayed as she had for the past four years. With the mid-day news reporting a thirteen-year-old girl in Indianapolis had been rescued from a human trafficking ring, Meera's story hit closer to home than ever before.

"Mom!" Lily's voice called her back to the present. The screen door slammed. "Mom!"

"Lillian Elisabeth Michael, you do not need to yell and you certainly don't need to slam the door."

"Sorry, Mom, but I was looking for you. Can I go over to Kendall's house? She has new puppies."

Beth looked at the clock. "It will have to wait. Dinner is in an hour and I don't have time to drive you there."

"I could walk, Mom. It's only around the block."

"You're not walking there by yourself, Lily."

"But Mom! That's not fair!"

Beth put her hands on her hips. "Are you talking back to me? Are you saying you never want to see those puppies?"

Lily's shoulders sagged. "No, ma'am. It's just that I don't understand."

Beth crossed the room and put her arm around her daughter. "I know you don't understand, sweetie. Sometimes you have to trust me. I have my reasons. I can't drive you right now. I have to get dinner on the table. And we have a hard and fast rule about you walking somewhere by yourself, right?"

"Yes, ma'am."

"Here." Beth held out the paper napkins. "You fold these and help me set the table and we'll see about going to see the puppies after dinner, okay?"

Lily's face brightened. "Okay."

Beth watched as her eldest methodically folded the napkins into soft, white triangles. *Sometimes you have to trust me.* "I get it, God. I want to trust You all the time. Not just sometimes," she whispered as she pulled the chicken from the refrigerator.

Chapter 10

Walnut Hills, Cincinnati, Ohio
Autumn

Catharine pushed the crock of honey toward her sister. "I refuse to serve sugar, as it comes to me by way of a poor slave's hands.

"Thank you." Harriet poured herself a second cup of tea. "I had another dream last night."

"These dreams haunt you, Harriet. Have you told Calvin about them?"

"I try not to do so. He once suggested they are the result of a malady of some sort. I don't think the man has ever had a dream in his life." Harriet stirred the honey in her tea and seated herself near the window in the kitchen.

"Still..."

Harriet took her sister's hand. "Do not fret over me, Catharine. The dream doesn't haunt me as you say. I merely seek to know what to do with it."

"Write it down."

"What?" Harriet put her cup down. "Commit it to paper? I think not."

"You must. Don't you see, dear sister, its meaning will never be clear to you until you preserve it. Add to it when you must. But it will leave you not. Nor will its meaning be revealed until you write it down."

Harriet allowed her sister's words to sink in. To commit it to paper gave her a chill. *How will I ever rid myself of it if it is forever inked on parchment?* "But Catharine, I fear writing it down. Once it is written, it will never die."

Catharine leaned back in the chair and crossed her arms. "Then we shall kill it."

"What?"

"Write the dream down. If in doing so our Lord reveals the meaning to you, so be it. If not, we burn it, never to be read or considered again."

"Like the time Charles wrote that music piece and upon its completion, Father made him burn the composition?" Harriet suggested.

"Exactly! Father bellowed out that such music was surely the tool of Satan himself, but he allowed Charles to write it down…"

"Then made him destroy the entire piece. I remember. Never again did we hear anything like it." Harriet's shoulders relaxed. "When I wake, I only remember bits and pieces of the dream. Perhaps if I collect them all, I shall be able to put them together and fathom its meaning." She stood. "But for today I must see to the completion of a piece I call *Parents and Children*. I've committed it to the *New York Observer and Chronicle*.

Chapter 11

Mt. Adams, Cincinnati
Late Autumn

Beth whispered a prayer as she hit the button marked "accept" to join the Zoom meeting. Grateful John prayed with her before leaving for the university this morning, and armed with a list of reasons supporting the project she wanted to tackle next, Beth put on her best smile when her agent, Angela Parks popped up on the screen.

"Hey, girl!"

"Good morning, Angie. How's everything with you?"

"Oh, you know, busy as usual. Nancy loved your latest manuscript. I told her you're roughly halfway through the final book for that series. She's already asking what's next."

"Yeah, about that. I have a book in mind. A standalone. It's one I've been mulling over and actually praying about for a few years now. I think this is the time."

The pause on the line meant Angie's wheels were turning. Hopefully in the right direction.

"A standalone. Well, of course you can write a standalone. Your first two romances are still going strong. Yes, a standalone. A break from the series stuff. I get it. Back to basics."

Angie was struggling to understand and sound supportive. Beth could hear it in her voice. *Of course I can write a standalone? I don't need your permission.*

"Look, I know we talked about the Tarpon Springs series in Florida. I still have notes and ideas for that, but I need to get this book that rolls around in my head on paper."

"I understand. It's just that I kind of started shopping the Florida series around to a couple of publishers."

"What happened with Buzz Lightyear?" The image of the square-headed publisher popped in her mind.

"Beth, you really have to stop calling him that. One day I'm going to let it slip out and call him Buzz."

"Okay, okay, but why change publishers now? Buzz, I mean Aaron likes my work."

"Jim Livingston is considering a book and movie deal."

"With no manuscript in hand?"

Angie bit her lower lip. "I met him at a writing conference. We got to chatting. He's familiar with your work and talked about his connections in the movie industry."

"What movie connections?"

"He's worked a few deals. Actually, he's into the sort of 'made for TV' movies. But Beth, it's a huge market."

"Well, I own the rights to my first two novels. If you want to pitch one of those to this guy, go for it. But my next new book is important to me. I'm not knocking out another cozy mystery just yet."

Chapter 12

Walnut Hills, Cincinnati, Ohio
Autumn, 1847

Harriet placed her hand to her stomach. She drew in a deep breath at the familiar flutter of the child within.

"You seem quite content to bear a sixth child, sister."

Harriet put her finger to her lips. "Shhh…I have yet to tell the children."

Catharine grinned. "Wait much longer and you need not say a word. Honestly, Harriet, I can see your clothes bulging even now."

Harriet looked down. "My garments may be a bit snug, but not uncomfortably so. Not yet."

"And the dresses I adapted for you?"

"I believe there may be one or two in a trunk in the attic. I gave the brown dress and the green one to Samantha Bingham and she's since moved."

"Well, perhaps I'll have Calvin retrieve the trunk and ensure the dresses are mended, laundered, and ready for you."

Harriet carried the sweet biscuits to the table and sat down next to her sister. "Would you like more coffee?"

"I think not. I have much to do this morning at Father's house. I only came because you've been ill."

"I think that time of sickness has passed. I seem to have more energy with this one than with any of the others. Perhaps it is because of my improved health overall."

"Then you shall be at the Semicolon meeting tonight?"

"Indeed. I've written an article for the cause I wish to put forth."

Catharine laughed. "Dear sister, here I am with only the charge to educate children and prepare a meal now and then for Father and have nothing written for the writing club. You manage this household, have five, soon to be six children and a husband and write more than any of us."

"Your recipes and household information are the only reason any of us manage our personal lives at all. And where would the school be without your textbooks? I may publish more than you, dear sister, but because of the education you champion for women and your model of using the printed word, lives are changed."

Catharine leaned back in her chair. "Well, now that we've suitably commended one another, I suggest we move forward with our day. I'll get my bonnet. I promised the children the library today and so it shall be. But first I must see to my morning duties at Father's house." She stood. "Unless you need me here."

"Oh, posh!" Harriet waved her hand aside. "We are fine. I'll have the children ready, save Georgie. She and I will treasure the day alone, I assure you. I think we will go for a walk in the park."

Harriet watched as her sister walked up the hill leading to their father's home. She put her hand on her stomach. "Where will you be born, little one? Here or at Father's house?" The memory of birthing her children at the house on Gilbert Avenue was sweet, but the cause for doing so weighed heavy. *If Calvin were to be called away to raise money or anything else for the school when this one is born...* Harriet let the thought drift away. After all, this one should arrive in January. Winter was hardly the time for raising funds. And it was certainly not the ideal time for recruiting the next class of students.

Chapter 13

Mt. Adams, Cincinnati, Ohio
November

"Angie? It's Beth."

"How's my favorite author?"

Beth sat down on the living room sofa with her phone and glanced at the clock. Iris wouldn't awake from her nap for another thirty or forty minutes. "I'm fine. And you?"

"Great. I just sent the galleys back to Ian. He's handling the cover art for the River series. Everything looks good and I got your message that the last book is nearly ready for a first read. You amaze me, Beth. You're turning into a writing machine."

"Well, I don't know about that, but I wanted to officially share my decision with you. I'm not pitching another series yet. They're all starting to sound the same to me anyway. Like a cake recipe where you simply substitute chocolate for vanilla or something."

Silence on the line. Beth held her breath.

"I've prayed about this, Beth, and I need you to understand something."

Uh-oh, here she goes. Some pitch to try to make me feel guilty about changing up what I write. "Okay…"

"Remember when you and I started working together and we prayed over each and every book?"

"I remember." *Brace yourself, Elisabeth.*

"We were both in it to bring honor and glory to God. I think we've done that, but I also think we kind of got ourselves lost along the way."

Beth narrowed her brows. "What do you mean?"

"Oh, Beth, I'm not saying we did anything wrong, we both just lost sight of why we were in this writing game in the first place."

Beth heard her agent draw in a deep breath.

"I've started praying about your next book. Not that it gets to me on time or that it is a best seller, or we get a movie contract out of it or anything like that. I've been praying for you. Praying God will direct your crafting of this book and that it will be one that does more than entertain. I'm praying it will change lives."

"Oh, Angie!" The emotion in Beth's voice startled even her. "You have no idea what your support means to me. I felt as if I would be letting you down if I didn't keep a string of popular cozies churned out."

Chapter 14

Walnut Hills, Cincinnati, Ohio
November 1847

"Though I enjoy the fresh garden vegetables immensely, I must say the endless cleaning of beans to dry for later wears on the spirit. Though now that the chill is in the air, the beans will be a tasty treat," Harriet commented to Catharine as they sat working in her kitchen.

"You will have many a delicious meal in the winter. I believe we dried enough beans for entire city of Cincinnati! And, Harriet, I always think how good it is to not have to traipse out in the garden to pick beans as we do all summer."

"Catharine, you are good for me. I fear I quite often get lost in the tedious routines of the day. You always seem to see a distant light to guide your actions."

"'Tis only practice, dear sister. Remember, I am nearly a dozen years your senior. Practice breeds patience."

"Still, I should rather be writing this afternoon than cooking. I am preparing something for the *Christian Watchman* and working on a story I call *Feelings* for the *Lady's Book*. I have every indication both will find an audience before this little one arrives." Harriet rested her small hand on her abdomen."

Catharine smiled. "Have you a thought as to whether it is a boy or a girl?"

"Though I try not to reflect upon it, I share with you, and you alone, dear sister, that I believe this child to be a boy. Do not ask me why. I have no evidence for making such a prediction. I simply feel it is that way." Harriet tossed a handful of beans into the bowl on the table.

"I can finish these, if you like. I tend to write by lamplight. It is the best time to pick up my pen."

"No, Catharine. I will help. I treasure our conversations, and as the boiling of beans and preparing the evening meal requires no thought, we can discuss anything you like. The children won't interrupt us for fear of being put to work."

"Indeed! So tell me about this story of yours. What did you call it? Feelings?"

Chapter 15

Mt. Adams, Cincinnati, Ohio
January

John put the last of the ornaments in a box. "I know you love decorating for Christmas, but I'm the one who winds up putting everything away."

"Hah, I help!" Beth retorted. "Anyway, you have to admit it feels crisp and clean once all the clutter of the holiday is gone."

"Wait a minute. As I recall, you told me how all the decorations made you feel so wonderful. That was your argument to get me to help you put everything up. Remember?"

Beth shrugged. "What can I say? Different seasons, different feelings."

"Yeah, well, I'm ready for an entirely new season."

"Spring is a few months off, you know." She put the last strip of packing tape on the ornament box.

"I was thinking more college football bowl games. 'Tis the season."

Beth let out a loud sigh. "There's always a sport season in your book."

"Just the way I'm wired, babe."

"Well, help me get this stuff back up into the attic and I'll heat us up some of last night's chili and you can watch the sports station to your heart's content."

"That's a deal. Only, since the kids are at your mom's for the evening, I could be convinced to do a bit of snuggling before the game starts."

Beth grinned and put her arms around John. "Now that's what I call a deal." She looked up in time to meet him with a kiss.

Chapter 16

Walnut Hills, Cincinnati, Ohio
January 1848

"There is most often a settling after Christmastime. Yet I am weary. Even as we spoke of Mary, laden with carrying the Christ child, I felt surely the Lord made her burden less. I could not help but wonder if she felt as cumbersome as I," Harriet commented, looking around the bedroom in her father's house.

"There, there," Lydia said softly. "It is good you've come to stay here. Your father and I welcome the opportunity to serve you, and the midwife you've engaged is delightful."

Harriet squirmed in the bed, trying to get comfortable. "Where is this delightful midwife right now?"

"I believe she is in the kitchen." Lydia looked at her stepdaughter. "You're frowning, dear. Are you in pain?"

"Indeed!"

"Oh, my, I shall fetch the girl at once."

Harriet struggled to find comfort. Her back ached. Sharp pains encircled her abdomen. Beads of perspiration circled her head.

"Miss Harriet?" the young woman called to her.

Harriet stared. "You're not Mrs. Crosley."

"No, ma'am. I'm her daughter. I'm trained well enough. Mother was at the Fulbright house when your son came. He's headed there now. I came to see if I could be of service until Mother arrives."

"This is my sixth child. Five pregnancies and six children. Each coming a moment faster than the others as if it were a race. I sincerely doubt, Miss…whatever your name is…that your mother will arrive on time."

The girl dampened a cloth and placed it on Harriet's head. "That may be, Mrs. Stowe, but I trust you and I, with God's help, will get this job done. I'll need to check things, though. Is that suitable to you?" The girl sounded calm.

"What is your name?"

"Maisy."

"Well, Maisy, I suppose you are right."

Dorthea Crosley appeared at the door moments after the child made his appearance. "Looks like I'm a bit late. But it looks, too, that my daughter handled everything quite well."

Harriet looked up from the bundle in her arms to Mrs. Crosley. "Let's put it this way, Mrs. Crosley, had this one been a girl, I would have been inclined to name her Maisy."

"Ah, yes Maisy would not be a suitable name for a boy. What will you call him?"

"We decided to call him Samuel Charles Stowe," Harriet said. She looked into the angelic face of her infant son. "My Charley."

Chapter 17

Mt. Adams, Cincinnati, Ohio
January

"I sent it off," Beth announced to her family as she walked into the family room.

"Sent what off, Mommy?" Violet asked.

"Her book," Iris said. "She always gets excited when she finishes writing a book."

"Oh, I thought maybe you ordered something for me." Violet settled back into the cushion she appropriated for watching the video they selected for family night.

"Hey kiddos, don't be so rough on me. I'm finished and that means I'm making popcorn and joining all of you for the movie."

"With butter?" Violet asked.

Beth nodded. "Extra butter."

"Yay," the girls squealed.

John followed Beth into the kitchen. "The short story for Plot Twisters?"

"Yep. And now I can tackle the project I've been mulling over for the last few years."

John put his arms around Beth and drew her close as the popcorn began to make popping sounds in the microwave. "I know this next book is important to you so it's important to me as well. But honey..." John's voice trailed off.

Beth pushed back away from her husband's chest. "'But honey...' what?"

"Human trafficking is a dark hole to descend. I want you to know I'm here for you. I want you to not rush this and get into a place that, well, ..."

"Well, what?"

"I love you. I want you to write this because it needs to be written and obviously, God chose you to do it. But I want you to take extra good care of yourself as you climb down into that dark dungeon. You won't feel as free to talk about it at mealtime or while the girls are in the room. Does any of this make sense?"

Beth wrapped her arms around John and nuzzled into his chest. "More than you know. John Michael, I love you. I'm still not sure the angle I'll take or if it will even amount to anything, but I hope to start the research next week."

Chapter 18

Walnut Hills, Cincinnati, Ohio
Early Summer, 1849

Charley toddled in the garden. At nearly eighteen months old, he was surprisingly agile. Harriet delighted in the newest member of the family.

"I call him my Sunshine Child," she told her sister one afternoon.

"All of your children are like a ray of sunshine to me, Harriet."

"You serve us all, Catharine, yet never married, nor have you ever expressed an interest in raising up a family of your own."

"As you know, dear sister, I hold to a philosophy of both independence and usefulness, both of which I could nary navigate as well as you do if I had children of my own. I am instead blessed to be the aunt your children need.

"I fear we put far more on you than you should shoulder."

"Not at all." Catharine adjusted her bonnet. "I reap the benefits of having a houseful of children without the responsibility of waking up in the middle of the night to feed one or comfort another."

Harriet started to laugh, but caught herself. "That would be humorous to me if I weren't so tired from being up last night with Charley. I believe he is catching a cold. I thought the fresh air might serve him well."

Chapter 19

Walnut Hills, Cincinnati, Ohio
Late Summer, 1849

"Oh, Lord, I cannot fathom this moment. My dear Charley. My Sunshine Child. The grief is too much to bear. The depth of despair lies beyond my comprehension. Oh that You, my Lord God, would have taken me instead. How can this be? A babe. A little child. Yes, Father God, You know this pain. Thine own Son was brutally killed before Thine eyes. Oh that Thou wouldst reach down from Thy throne in heaven and comfort me in this loss. Oh that Thou wouldst lift this crushing pain from my breast."

Harriet opened the Bible on her lap. She began reading. Verses in the Book of Proverbs jumped off the page and into her heart. She read them again. And again. Finally, Harriet pulled the strength to speak the words aloud into the quiet confines of her bedroom.

"Trust in the Lord with all thine heart; and lean not unto thine own understanding. In all thy ways acknowledge Him, and He shall direct thy paths."

She read the verses once more before squeezing her eyes closed, lest yet another tear escape. "I do not understand, Lord. I shall acknowledge Thee. I shall not cease to praise Thee in Thy wisdom and mercy. Yea, Lord, I shall need Thy strength for mine is spent. Thy strength. I shall do all within my grasp to trust Thee, my God. My Lord. My Savior. I shall do all within my being to follow Thy direction."

"Mother?"

Harriet turned to see her seven-year-old standing in the doorway. She wiped the tears from her eyes. "Yes, Georgie?"

"Mother, I'm sorry you are so sad about Charley. Papa said he's in heaven. Papa said that heaven is better than earth so I'm sorry he's not here anymore but I'm glad he got to go to someplace even more beautiful and better."

Harriet smiled and Georgiana flew into her mother's open arms. "My sweet Georgie. You are but a messenger of truth. And with truth, my child, comes hope."

The summer sun streamed through the thick windowpane, casting an array of color on the walls. Georgie pushed away. "Look, Mother! Rainbows! Aunt Catharine says rainbows are God's promise of life."

"Indeed they are." Harriet hugged her young daughter close. "Do you know the story of Noah and the Ark?"

"Yes, Mother. Noah gathered the animals and saved them from the flood."

"True. But there is always more to the story than meets the eye. God placed a rainbow in the sky as a promise to Noah." Harriet rocked her daughter back and forth on her lap. "It seems in our darkest times, God reminds us He is there."

"Mother, I think God gave us these rainbows to remind us again. We need to be reminded, don't we, Mother?"

Harriet set Georgie down on the floor, stood and straightened herself. "Indeed we do, my sweet one. Indeed we do. We tend to forget when times are dark that God is still God and light will come to us again."

Chapter 20

Mt. Adams, Cincinnati, Ohio
Late Summer

Beth held the blue striped hoodie up for inspection. The weight was perfect for Iris. "It may look a bit boyish but it would be comfortable. What do you think, sweetie?"

Iris arched her back in the seat of the shopping cart and tried to reach the stuffed clown she'd dropped in the basket. "Tuna!" she called.

Beth dropped the hoodie in the cart and reached for the stuffed toy. "I have no idea where you got the name Tuna for that ratty looking clown." She looked up as Iris straightened up in the seat. "Violet?" She looked behind her. "Violet?" Her voice was gaining strength.

"Violet!" Beth lifted Iris from cart and started through the store, calling out to her middle child at an ever-increasing volume. "Violet!"

A clerk with an armful of garments walked toward her. "Is there something wrong?"

"Something? My eight-year-old daughter's missing. She was just here a minute ago. Her name is Violet. Please lock the doors or something."

"She's probably hiding under one of the racks," the woman said.

"Look..." Beth read the nametag on the woman's shirt. "Jen. My daughter is missing. She is a little girl. Please help me!" Beth could hear the shakiness in her voice and the volume increase with every word. She didn't care. "Violet!" she shouted at the top of her lungs.

"What's the matter, Mommy?"

Beth turned to see her daughter standing behind her, wide-eyed and shaking. "Are you okay?" Beth knelt down, balancing Iris on one knee and pulling Violet toward her.

"I'm okay, Mommy. Why are you crying?"

Because there are evil people in this world who snatch beautiful little girls away from their families. "Because I couldn't find you, sweetheart. Where were you? Didn't you hear me call your name?"

Chapter 21

Brunswick, Maine
Spring, 1851

Unbidden, the dream returned. Harriet woke with a start.

"The dream was different this time, Calvin," she admitted to her husband at breakfast. "And it was real."

"Real?"

"I suppose I had pushed it out of my mind, but yes, those things really happened. I remember that summer so well. Marshall Key supported the school in every way. He was a widower with a daughter named Elizabeth. He invited two other girls from the seminary and myself to their home in Washington, Kentucky.

"I remember the room where I stayed. The bed was of the deepest, softest down I ever knew. I remember the shadows of the cool night coming through the window. I stood at that very window the following morning and listened to the sounds of the town waking from a summer slumber."

Calvin put his hand out for his wife. "Go on."

"I could hear the rhythmic sounds of a man's voice across the square. At first, I thought it to be a preacher but then I realized it was an auctioneer. I had seen a whole house of furniture auctioned in Connecticut to lay account for the misfortune of a rather unlucky businessman. I remember thinking about that as I dressed."

"What happened next, dear wife?"

"After we had dressed and had eaten breakfast, we started off to tour the town square." Harriet shuddered. "They were not auctioning things, but rather people. One woman, with coffee colored skin was there. A man grabbed her and…"

Calvin squeezed Harriet's hand. "It's all right. You need not say more."

Harriet looked into his kind eyes. "But I must." She drew in a deep breath. "Calvin, the man grabbed her whilst another pulled a young child from her arms." Harriet swallowed hard at the memory. "She cried for her child. She begged for the little one."

"She was sold?"

"Yes. Sold. Not as a person but as a thing. Something to be owned and used and tossed aside. And then--" Harriet reached deep for some inner strength to speak the words. "And then her child was next on the auctioneer's block."

Calvin swallowed hard. "We really don't know what it's like, do we." It was more a statement than a question.

The two sat in silence for a moment before Harriet answered, "I think I do."

Calvin's eyes studied those of his wife.

"I do know what it is like to have a child ripped from your arms. You do, too." Harriet touched the locket around her neck. Opened, one side revealed the image of her Sunshine Child. The other, a lock of his hair.

Calvin drew in a deep breath and fought the tears that threatened to make him appear less a man. "Our Charley."

The two sat in silence at the breakfast table as the coffee cooled and the biscuits remained untouched. Only the sound of the children stirring in the rooms above them brought them back to the day at hand. Calvin stood, kissed Harriet's forehead and whispered a prayer in her ear.

The realization of the dream haunted her as she performed the morning rituals of care for her children and readied them for their schooling. Once the children were set in their books, Harriet retreated to the drawing room, pulled out pen and paper from her writing box and began a letter to her editor.

"Dear Mr. Bailey..."

Chapter 22

Mt. Adams, Cincinnati, Ohio
Spring

Beth put her jacket on the hook behind the kitchen door and instructed Lily to take her things upstairs.

"So how'd it go?" John asked.

"I have to say, it was well received and Lily seemed to enjoy the whole event. She was the only child in the group, so everyone made a fuss over her. I'm sorry you couldn't be there. How's Violet feeling?"

"Better." He looked at his watch. "She hasn't thrown up again since you left, and she fell asleep about an hour ago."

"I hate it when one of the kids gets sick." Beth kicked off her shoes and settled in beside her husband. "John, you know how I've struggled to write Meera's story?"

"Uh-huh." He put his book aside, wrapped his arm around her and drew her close. "And?"

"Well, I took your advice and finished the series and now I've finished the story for the anthology. It took some research to find the right angle to write a contemporary story including an historical figure like Harriet Beecher Stowe, you know."

John nodded. "Last I heard you were having your contemporary character use some recipe of Stowe's. Is that still on?"

"That's what I wrote for the group project. At least part of it. But, honey, there was something else that happened and it hit home tonight as I did the presentation for the Plot Twisters." Beth shifted on the couch, turned toward John and pulled her feet up under her. "I think I was trying so hard to make something work, I almost missed the most amazing piece."

"I'm listening."

"Well," Beth began. "It kind of all came together when Violet threw up."

John frowned. "Go on."

"Sorry. It wasn't that she got sick exactly, but as I shared my presentation to the group, it all sort of made sense." She bit her bottom lip and stared a moment toward the window. "I hadn't exactly put it all into words until tonight. You see, Harriet Beecher Stowe wrote all sorts of stories and biblical studies, and articles. And of course, the recipes I told you about. She was getting published but still waiting for God to show her what He needed her to write."

"*Uncle Tom's Cabin*, right?"

"Right. She honed her writing in every direction, but the story in her heart wasn't a story really, it was a cause. *Uncle Tom's Cabin* was her way to help people see slavery for what it was. To live it.

To feel it."

"I understand."

"Well, first of all, the Stowes had seven children in all. They had twin girls and then two boys, another daughter, then another son. Then later a seventh child who was also a son. Following me?"

"Maybe…"

"Anyway, the sixth child, a boy, was born in 1848. His name was Samuel Charles, but they called him Charley. Harriet called him her Sunshine Child. I think that's because the others were born about every two years and he came along five years after their daughter Georgiana."

"You're losing me here."

"Just listen. Charley was born in Cincinnati in January of 1848, but became ill and died in July of 1849 of cholera. That had to be devastating."

"I agree."

"They moved from Cincinnati after his death to Maine. Anyway, when Stowe was younger, before marrying Calvin, she had visited a place in Kentucky with a young woman from the seminary. She witnessed a slave auction and saw a slave child separated from the mother. They were sold separately, I think. At some point, Stowe wrote that the sorrow she felt in losing her son was bitter and reminded her of the slave woman who also had her child ripped from her arms.

"When I was doing my research, I came across a communication Harriet sent to the editor of a weekly anti-slavery journal called *The National Era*. The editor was a man by the name of Gamaliel Bailey. She wrote…wait a minute, I want to get this right." Beth opened her notebook and flipped through the pages. "Here it is. She wrote, 'I feel now that the time is come when even a woman or a child who can speak a word for freedom and humanity is bound to speak…I hope every woman who can write will not be silent.'"

John took the paper from her hand. "Every woman who can write…"

"I don't know fully how I will share Meera's experience. How she was ripped from her family and sold into the vile practice of human trafficking. I do know it is not limited to India and it is a story God has put on my heart to write."

John looked into Beth's eyes. "Did your research reveal how Mrs. Stowe's husband responded to her?"

Beth frowned. "No, but..."

John put his finger on her lips. "Shhh...I don't know that it is recorded, but if he felt in any way as I do at this moment, he said something along the lines of 'I am honored to call you my wife.'"

END

Author's Note: *When our writing group decided to explore sites on the Ohio Literary Trail, I chose to host a visit of the Harriet Beecher Stowe House, located in the neighborhood of Walnut Hills in Cincinnati. Though fictionalized, the Harriet Beecher Stowe story is based on careful research of the over twenty years she resided in Cincinnati.*

Beth Michael is a purely fictional character but her passion to help bring human trafficking to light and to an end is one I share with her. In 2015, I had the opportunity to work with survivors of this heinous practice of modern-day slavery in India. The realization that this evil exists here in the United States horrifies me. Together we can bring human trafficking to an end.

Rebecca Waters is both an author and speaker. Visit her website at www.WatersWords.com. *Her latest release,* Writing to Publish, *is a compilation of presentations, blog posts, and journal articles offered to help writers reach their publishing goals.*

THE MASK
By Betty Kulich

Chapter 1
Reminiscing

Early Hours of New Year's Day, 1900
*House of Four Pillars**
Toledo Area, Ohio

If You Dare
Wear it if you dare – Wear it and become fair.
Wear it if you suffer – Wear it as your buffer.
Through new eyes you will see – just who God created you to be.
Watch what a new view will do – Transformation into the new you.
Trust the Mask and lose the past.
Life will take on purpose and meaning – The truths of life will reveal
*   your inner being.*
Time and circumstances brought the Mask to your hand –
Wear it and find your special Godly man.
His love will forever be only for you – Trust the Mask and say, "I
*   do."*
Love awaits, make no mistake
The passing of time has brought your season –
To move forward, you must give up logic and reason.

Clarissa's eyes teared up as she finished reading the poem one last time. Long ago she followed the poem's advice and found her true, lasting love. God's hand had indeed brought her the Mask and the Mask altered the course of her life. New tears welled up in her eyes as she remembered her husband of almost forty-eight years. Charles had died three months ago, and her loss was still fresh. He had quietly passed in his sleep in October, just four days shy of his eighty-second birthday – rare age for the times. But God had been good to them in sickness, health, finances and all the aspects of life. Only the blessing of children had been elusive, a result of an injury sustained on the second day of the Battle at Vicksburg. It had sent Charles to a field hospital until he was well enough to travel back to the front. The wound earned him the rank of Major General.

The striking of the clock signaled midnight, launching a new century. New Year's Eve was laden with sweet memories. Clarissa pulled herself back from the past and rolled the poem carefully into a cylinder, so the delicate parchment didn't break. Only God knew how old the parchment and poem were. The stories from the "passenger" claimed it had been passed down through the centuries from the Queen of Sheba, a wedding gift from King Solomon. The Queen's tribe passed it to the first-born girl of each reigning chief. The poem and the Mask it accompanied had been a precious gift that needed to be passed on to someone God would choose. Since she never had children, Clarissa trusted that through time, the Mask and scroll would come to the special one God intended to bless. With renewed purpose she retied the claret silk ribbon into a perfect bow, securing the scroll.

"Well, may you find your place of purpose, and impact another life for good," Clarissa declared out loud with a smile, laughter in her aging voice as she held up the rolled scroll, as if making a covenant with God.

She placed the scroll neatly inside the white woolen pouch that protected the piece of hand-tatted silk lace that made up the Mask. Although centuries old, the Mask was still the purest of white. No yellowing of time marred the Mask or the pouch. No one would ever suspect the tatted lace was a life-changing, destiny-creating Mask. The woolen pouch was then placed tenderly inside the folds of her wedding gown. The gown was yellowed with age, with a waist that would not fit her now, even with a corset. Closing the lid of the Saratoga trunk with a *thunk* brought an ending to a part of her life that had been changed forever by the gift of the Mask.

Clarissa felt suddenly tired and sank into the velvet Victorian stuffed chair. Her mind traveled quickly back to the day when her life changed. She pictured it like a Magic Lantern show but with colored slides. The night winds had been howling, the icy rain had pelted her skin, stinging like hundreds of bee stings as she had made her way down the ravine towards the Maumee River so many years ago. No one would ever imagine the events following that fate-filled night and how they changed her life forever.

Maybe I should write out my story and put it with the scroll. It might encourage the next recipient God has intended for the Mask.

Clarissa made a mental note to start creating a journal the next day, noting the unbelievable events caused by the Mask. Pushing her aging body slowly out of the chair, she headed to bed. It would be her first night not wearing the Mask in forty-nine years. She could feel the difference. She knew looking into the mirror she would look different, old, and wrinkled. But wearing her black mourning veil would transition her appearance from the ageless, flawless beauty the Mask had created to her now-aging face. Everyone would believe the changes to her looks were the result of mourning her beloved husband. She still had more than a year and a half to don her black garments, veil, and jewelry. Clarissa smiled. Her secret would go to the grave with her.

Spring, Present
House of Russell and Louise Rush, Janet's Parents

Cleaning out the attic for her parents' downsizing move was proving to be mundane and tiresome. But Janet persevered and was down to the last corner of the attic. Shoved back into the eave, a sheet covered an old, domed Saratoga trunk. A beveled oval mirror stood behind it. Out from the sheet covering the trunk peeked glimpses of tarnished metal, wood, and leather straps. The trunk seemed to call for her to touch it. She was intrigued — fascinated as her hands were drawn to feel its texture beneath the sheet. Her imagination was suddenly captivated with vivid flashes of possible past lives flashing onto the screen of her mind as her fingertips made contact.

What a strange reaction to a dusty old trunk! Now what could be in here? Janet wondered as she pulled the sheet from the trunk, almost causing a shoebox of old pictures to slide off.

Dancing in the sunbeams from the dormer window, particles of dust, dead flies and ladybug shells cluttered the air, settling down on every surface. Janet sneezed and rubbed her nose as she peered for the first time upon the exposed trunk. It looked as though it could have come from a carriage excursion to some faraway place.

Wouldn't it be lovely to escape on an adventure accompanied by a trunk full of petticoats, ball gowns and boas? Oh, and don't forget the shoes, hats, and parasols. Smiling, Janet shook her head to clear her strange and sudden fantasy. *Where did that thought come from? What is it all about? I'm a practical gal and there's no room for a life full of delights and adventures.*

But her fascination was pulled right back to what might be hidden inside, possibly something wrapped in yellowing paper. Maybe it contained a sleeveless flapper dress full of beaded tassels, revealing scandalous knees, elbow-length matching gloves, beaded headband, strapped pumps, and long cigarette holder. Janet giggled and shook her head. The heat of the attic, ignoring lunch, and lack of hydration was now getting to her. It was a good thing she was nearly finished.

Kneeling, Janet reached to touch the center lock, hoping it opened. She needed to quickly finish exploring and sorting what should go to her parents' downsized condo. The rest would go to the church bazaar fundraiser to build accessible restrooms. She tried lifting the lock as she squeezed the rusty buttons on each side of the keyhole. Nothing moved. She was done. It needed a key.

She pushed her matted, sweaty hair from her face as she stood, glancing at herself in the dressing mirror standing behind the trunk. Greyish streaks of dust and sweat were smeared across her cheeks and forehead. Cobwebs and ladybug wings were stuck in her hair. The reflection showed her unremarkable features—her plain, limp brown hair made her twenty-six years look closer to forty.

"Mom!?" Janet yelled as she prepared to climb down the ladder from the attic. She turned to place her foot on the ladder and glanced back at the trunk that had so quickly captivated her. For a brief second, she thought a light was peeking out around the edge of the lid. It was as if a glittery glow beckoned from the trunk to connect her with something inside. She blinked, thinking it was the floating dust still in the sunlit air, but the glow was gone.

Climbing down the ladder she continued to yell, "I found an old trunk from the Civil War era and it's the last thing I need to go through, so you and Dad can clean out the attic. Ninety-nine percent of what's up there is stuff to go to the church's bazaar.

There was nothing of value except that old trunk and what may be in it."

By now Janet's mom was upstairs. She smiled as she wiped some grey dust from her daughter's sweaty cheek.

"You look worn out from that heat! Come, let's get you something to drink and I'll look for that key. I put out a clean washrag and towel so you can wipe down some before you head home."

Janet walked into the bathroom and smiled at the memories of her childhood in this home. She had been so happy here until …. the face of her one and only crush hovered like a hummingbird at the feeder of her mind. They had been childhood best buds from the time they were in Mrs. Grace's kindergarten class on through high school graduation. They had gone to all the parties, homecoming dances, and proms together. If there was a social event, they did it together. They were inseparable. Janet and most people had assumed that college wouldn't change anything, and marriage would follow. But it did change. Liam was offered a sports scholarship to a college on the West Coast, and Janet was staying home in the Midwest to go to the local university, studying fashion history and design. It took only one semester for Liam to decide that his life really didn't need Janet anymore. He needed to move on from the past, go forward — and Janet didn't fit into that picture any longer.

Shooing away the visions of Liam with his soft auburn curls and Irish dimples, Janet turned quickly to the sink and ran cool water on the washrag. She wiped the dirt, sweat, and cobwebs off her face and arms and used the hand towel to rub the cobwebs and ladybugs from her hair. The coolness brought refreshing, but thoughts of Liam flooded right back in. He had moved on and like it or not, so had she. Janet had come to see that a long history of deep friendship-based events was not the same as true love. Infatuation with a teenage dream had been based in a foolish understanding of real relationships. As hard as it had been to have her bubble broken by Liam's awakening to the reality of attraction and affection with someone else, Janet was sadly thankful. Life now was safe and predictable.

After she worked through the shock and embarrassment of her fantasy world breaking apart, Janet threw herself into her collegiate studies. A BS in fashion and retail studies and a master's degree in history and culture of fashion from The University of the Arts, London, had directed her focus to the legacy of historic costumes and textiles collection. The past was enduring. It was established and not changeable. She could rest in the comfort of it. The present and future were once again planned, and her career was set before her. Taking the new interning position at the Victoria and Albert Museum in London, England, would keep her busy into the future. Her parents were healthy and downsizing with years ahead of them to spend together, enjoying life. She envied their happiness. She had once had that with Liam and assumed her future would mirror her parents' marriage. Now she had come to see that dreaming was useless. Although a part of her ached for a great love like her parents, a long and adventurous life with the love of her heart, life seemed to prove that wasn't in the cards for her. With a shake of her head to scatter the dismal thoughts, Janet stepped out of the bathroom and headed downstairs.

As Janet appeared, her mother began reminiscing about the trunk. "I had totally forgotten about that trunk. I bought that trunk at an auction years ago before you were even born to help support The Ohio Historical Society. Remember how your dad and I volunteered all the time at the Ohio Historical Village? Well, they were raising funds for some very needed building updates on properties around Ohio. They had collected donations of antiques from philanthropic people from all over. Supposedly that trunk had been found in the attic of an old home that was on the Ohio Literary Trail up in Maumee. I think it was called the House of the Four Pillars or something like that. The trunk took my fancy and came with the oval mirror. Your dad bought it for me—it went for a pretty penny, I can tell you. But you know your dad. He saw how enamored I was with it and so he bought it. I was planning to clean it up, sit it at the foot of our bed and store your grandmother's quilts—but I never got around to it. In fact, I opened it only once to see what it contained."

Janet pondered her mother's words. Janet's love of history and preserving the past had come from her parents. No wonder she had been drawn to the trunk. It was an enchanting piece with bewitching possibilities for what might be discovered inside. She had been captivated as soon as the dust had settled, and she gazed upon it. History and culture clues from a long past era could lie inside, perfect for a collection at a museum. Although the trunk was in great shape, what might lie within had grabbed Janet's focus. Suddenly she felt energized.

"Mom, if you don't want the trunk and mirror, I'd love to have them. Do you remember what's inside of the trunk? If it has clothing, I'll see that it gets to the best museums for their safekeeping and display."

"Sure honey, there will not be room with the downsizing. I opened the trunk when we first brought it home. It's filled with a ladies' gown, gloves, and stuff. They were in great shape then, but I couldn't say now. They may be moth-riddled and the makings of mice nests. You're welcome to the trunk. I'll have your dad get it and the mirror down and bring them to your house after dinner. That way they don't get mixed in with the stuff for the church bazaar. The men from the church are coming first thing in the morning, so it's got to go tonight. I think I remember where I put the key."

Janet began to protest that her dad shouldn't be hefting the large trunk down the attic ladder. Both the trunk and the mirror were large and bulky. But her mom ignored her look and went right on. "It's no problem for your dad to get them down. I can help him, and afterwards we will be over with it and some pizza for dinner, so you don't have to cook tonight after that long hot day up in the attic."

"But Mom…"

"You know I won't take no for an answer. It's just the kind of hidden treasure you have always loved to find. I'm just glad we can bless you with it."

Janet's mom smiled as she finished the sentence and turned to go look for the key. "Russell," her voice to get her husband's attention, "I'm going to need your help, but pizza is part of the deal …" Her words dropped off as she turned the corner to the living room.

Janet knew it was useless to argue with her mom when she had a plan. The trunk was going to find a new home at her place tonight. She gathered her stuff and headed to the back door for home and a long hot shower before pizza and the mystery trunk showed up at her house.

Chapter 2
The Shifting of Possessions

February 14th, 1900
*House of Four Pillars**
Toledo, Ohio

Clarissa closed the journal and sighed. Writing her story down in a journal for the next recipient of the Mask had been pure inspiration. She left nothing out. She wanted the new recipient to know both the power of the Mask and its ability to change a life. She had detailed every dialog, every expression, every emotion of her life from the meeting of "the passenger" on that cold wintery night so long ago. Oh, how she had enjoyed reliving each of those days as she inscribed her journal entries. She had written for hours every day since she had taken off the Mask at the turn of the new century, and today on Valentine's Day she had ended the last entry with the burial of her beloved Charles and her decision to remove the Mask. Her urgent desire was to pass it on to some other woman waiting and hoping to experience true love. The Mask and its purpose to change destinies must continue.

"Annie!" Clarissa called her live-in helper to come.

"Coming Clarissa!" Annie replied as she scurried up the stairs.

Annie had been Clarissa's live-in helper ever since Charles had passed back in October. Although seventy-seven years old, Clarissa had been spry and seemed to be half her age. But since New Year's Day and a new century, accompanied by the removal of the Mask, Clarissa seemed to fade in strength and vigor a little more each day. Annie hurried into the room to see what Clarissa needed. She noticed the slump in Clarissa's demeanor.

"Annie, would you please take this journal and lay it in that trunk up in the attic on top of my wedding dress? Here is the key." Clarissa pulled a gold chain from her neck with the trunk key dangling and handed it to Annie. "Lock the trunk back please and place the key with my papers and things that are to go to my niece. I want to make sure she has access."

"Sure Clarissa. Why don't I help you take a nap. You look tired after a full morning of writing in that journal. You have labored at that every day for over a month. If it is finished, you deserve a good rest."

"That is a good idea. I do feel my age more and more. It seems like as I relived my memoirs, the years came flooding back to me. I must admit, I do feel really old right now."

Annie helped Clarissa go over to her Victorian daybed and covered her with a wool blanket as she snuggled down for the nap. She hurried up to the attic to open the trunk and place the journal inside just like Clarissa had asked. Annie wanted to get the key placed in the box of papers for the niece and get back to her surprise for Clarissa—a red velvet cake for their dinner tonight on Valentine's Day. It had been Charles and Clarissa's favorite. Little did she know that Clarissa would not awaken from her nap but had gone to heaven to meet Charles on the anniversary of their wedding.

Spring, Present
Janet's House

Janet drove to her apartment by autopilot. Her mind was bombarded by a myriad of thoughts! What type of clothing could be in the trunk and who had they belonged to? Had they been happy? Was there love and adventure in their life? What would she find in the trunk? Part of the imagery flitting across her mind seemed to be men who had hair or dimples like Liam's. She pushed the images out of her mind and focused on the possibilities of what was in that trunk. Little did she know what awaited her…

For a moment, thoughts had fluttered down like confetti on the stage of her mind. What if Liam's affections had stayed with her? Would her life have been different? Was there ever going to be a man to come along and sweep her off her feet? Could there be a man who loved and adored her just like the stories described in romance novels or bring her a love as wonderful as her parents' love? Would she ever be lucky in love and attract a mate who esteemed, loved, honored, and respected her?

Pulling into her driveway jerked her dreams back to reality. *I guess I'll never know if life could have been different.* Janet clicked the garage opener, waited as it went up, and pulled in. Yes, life had moved on and so must she.

Her parents showed up right on time with the trunk, mirror, and hot pizza, diverting her attention from her dismal thoughts. She had just enough time to shower and wash her hair. Her mother suggested putting the trunk at the foot of her bed and the mirror in the corner across from it. They both fit perfectly.

"Let's eat while the pizza's hot," her dad yelled as Janet's mother handed her the trunk key.

"I found the key. I hope you find some great things in the trunk."

Janet was unexpectedly drawn to go right then and open the trunk to see what was in it. But her dad was calling them to come and eat.

"Come on girls!!! Pizza's getting cold! I got the add-on special too! Double cheesy bread with extra marinara sauce. It's not good cold."

Janet and her mom laughed. The paper plates were passed out with slices of pizza and with the crusty ends of the cheesy bread going to her dad. Life was familiar and reliable. Janet smiled as they sat down on the island stools.

Janet's parents stayed a while after pizza and talked to Janet about their pending move and how excited they were to meet the new neighbors, fellow retirees now enjoying their new season of life. As her parents talked and shared, Janet found herself only half listening. Her mind kept flashing to the trunk sitting at the end of her bed, drawn by the allure of what might be inside. The yearning was even stronger than her joy in family togetherness.

"You are only half with us," her mom finally said. "Let's go Russell, and let the girl get some sleep."

Janet's mom was up and pulling her husband's arm as Janet realized what her mom said.

She apologized for being inattentive. "You don't need to rush off. I can sleep in tomorrow. Besides, when you move, you aren't going to be as easy to connect with like you are now, especially when you start galivanting with friends."

Her mom smiled. "Yes, but I can see that your body is here with us, but your mind is elsewhere. That was hot work today and you need rest. It won't be long, and you'll be the one far away in London working and busy putting together that themed masked ball fundraiser, procuring the wedding dresses for the new wing in the museum. That was such an inspired idea for the museum to have a wing featuring nothing but wedding dresses since Queen Victoria became the trendsetter for wedding dresses by wearing a white gown some 180 years ago. Now it's the traditional color for a bride to wear."

"Yes!" Janet replied. "The wing will be a great addition and I can't wait to begin traveling and meeting the Royal family's agents and taking care of the large collection of donations from the Royals themselves. I've got many of the fundraiser ball details already planned and under contract, such as the venue, the orchestra, and the hors d'oeuvres. The last detail is the guest list and what costume I will wear."

"Well, I know it will be great, darling, and you are the perfect one to plan this event. You will have to send me pictures," Janet's mom said as she herded Russell toward the back door and away from the pizza and cheesy bread remains.

"Bye!" Janet laughed as the door clicked shut. She looked around the kitchen table. Nothing needed to be put away tonight. The remaining few pieces of pizza would keep until morning when she had them with a glass of cold milk for breakfast. Her bed was calling and so was a peek into the trunk. Around her neck was the key to the trunk. It felt warm against her skin. *What could be in that trunk? Does it contain clothing? Love letters? What will I find?*

Walking toward her bedroom, Janet noticed a small glimmer of a night light. That was strange. Had her dad turned on the bed lamp and forgotten to turn it off when he brought the trunk upstairs? As she entered her dark room, she saw a strange glow emanating from the keyhole in the trunk, also reflected by the oval beveled mirror across from it. *What the heck? Now how did a flashlight get turned on and left in the trunk?*

Janet turned on the night light beside the bed, walked over to the trunk and knelt, putting her hands on the domed lid. The trunk lid felt warm. She tried the lock, and it was still tightly secured. *Mom and Dad must have had one last look inside before they gave it to me. Dad must have forgotten that he left a light inside before he locked it back.*

Removing the key from around her neck, Janet inserted it into the lock—the trunk opened effortlessly. Raising the domed lid expecting to find a flashlight, all she saw was yellowed muslin that covered what was beneath. *That's strange. No light inside the trunk.*

How mysterious. The glow of the bedstand light softened the muslin's color even more.

Janet gently lifted the yellowed muslin, discovering a leather-bound book secured by two attached leather cords tied in a bow. As she gently untied the bow, she wondered what the book contained. As she turned the leather cover, her eyes beheld beautiful cursive handwriting. It was a little hard to read in the dim light next to her bed, but she could make it out.

> *The Memoirs of Clarissa Gillmore*
> *Devoted wife of Major General, Charles Gilllmore*
> *January 2nd, 1890*
> *The House of Four Pillars*

The curiosity to turn the next page was great, but the desire to see the contents of the trunk was greater. With slow and methodical hands accustomed to working with historical clothing, Janet used the muslin to protect the historical contents from any oils on her hands. At work, she normally wore cotton gloves to handle historical items. The first article was a full-length white Brussels lace veil, still in perfect condition but now yellowed with age. It was secured with three tortoise shell combs handtied to the lace, and with a pearl headband attached. Janet closed the muslin material these items were wrapped in and laid it on the floor next to the trunk. *Definitely, post 1840, since white wedding apparel only came into fashion after Queen Victoria's wedding.*

Next, Janet pulled back more muslin and found jewelry, intricate dainty fans, a nosegay with flowers now in tiny, dried pieces, a small purse with pearls embroidered on the outside, and a lace parasol. She covered them back up and laid that pile next to the veil. She could tell the next layer was probably the wedding dress. Removing the muslin, she saw silk, satin, pearls, and ribbons decorating the yellowed but beautiful wedding dress. The dress must have had some attached crinolines because the heap filled most of the trunk. Janet covered the dress back up and gathered it in her arms, gently laying it also to the side of the trunk.

With the dress out, Janet could see there was one last muslin pile. She uncrossed the fabric and discovered a linen chemise, drawstring drawers trimmed in lace and ribbons, a whalebone corset, and some cotton petticoats. As she viewed these items, her fatigue overcame her curiosity and she longed for sleep. She quickly covered the items. Standing up, she grabbed the wedding dress bundle and put it into the security of the trunk. As she did so, there was the slightest sound of something hitting her wooden floor, but in the shadows, she didn't see anything. Carefully placing the rest of the treasures back into the trunk, she spied the leather journal. Instead of returning it to the trunk, she decided to read a few entries in bed since the sudden fatigue had left as suddenly as it had come. Shutting the trunk lid, Janet carried the journal to her nightstand and laid it beside the reading lamp. She quickly changed for bed and brushed her teeth, then turned the alarm off on her phone and climbed into bed. She picked up the journal, savoring the smooth leather cover. She would read just the first chapter and sleep in.

The bed felt like pure delight as she snuggled in and carefully opened the journal with great anticipation. What secrets did Clarissa Gillmore have to reveal?

Chapter 3
Destiny Bridges the Past and the Present

Midnight, The Present
Janet's House

Janet didn't know how many journal entries she had read. She had first been captivated by Clarissa, an only child who considered herself a spinster at twenty-seven and had decided to take over running of the family business. Jilted in love and afraid of heartbreak again, she had determined to move on. With her widower father ailing with another bout of malaria from the dreaded Great Black Swamp, Clarissa devoted herself to him and his business. Although by 1850 the swamp had been drained, her father had lingering issues with the malaria. Clarissa had stepped in to give direction to her father's shares in the first railroad to operate west of the Allegheny Mountains: the Toledo Erie and Kalamazoo. When steam engines replaced the horses, she encouraged her father to sell land that later became Toledo's rail terminal and port facility, giving them the financial ability to again invest in multiple railroad companies operating from Toledo. Toledo was becoming a major rail center in the United States with numerous passenger trains, thousands of rail cars carrying agricultural products, raw materials, and manufactured goods from all over the country, arriving and departing daily. Their wealth and influence grew, making Clarissa a big "catch" for young men looking to marry for money. She was quick to sniff them out and catch them in their schemes. Many a suitor thought they would win her heart. Little did they know she just wasn't interested in a loveless marriage. Being a spinster and the one in control of her destiny was looking more like the ideal life.

Much like Clarissa, Janet had had a broken-heart relationship. Instead of languishing away, she turned her focus and energy into building a career that could take her all over the world. Janet could relate to a woman very much like herself—unmarried and determined to make a difference. Janet, like Clarissa would never marry, because finding the man who loved as completely as she did was not possible.

On Janet read, eagerly turning page after page in the journal, taken in by Clarissa's life and her ability to run a successful business in a day when men ruled the business world.

Then the story took on a different tone. Clarissa and her father had been greatly affected by the plight of the African slaves. They just couldn't understand how another human could treat someone like the stories they had heard firsthand. Clarissa's father had a great friend named John Rankin, a Presbyterian minister and abolitionist. He lived at the other end of the state from Clarissa and her father, but the two men had kept in contact. Though slavery was illegal at that time in Ohio, the passing of the Fugitive Slave Law of 1850 enabled ruthless bounty hunters to come up into Ohio and catch runaway slaves from the South. The slaves needed to escape the United States and flee to Canada, however possible. If caught, they were beaten, raped, and treated worse than a dog. It was also known that if the bounty hunters couldn't find their quota of escaped slaves, they would simply kidnap a free black man from the North and take him back instead.

In early fall of 1848, Clarissa and her father had traveled down to Ripley to spend a few days with John and Jean and their many children. Clarissa's dad wanted to see firsthand the operation called the Underground Railroad. He had been considering making his house a part of the Underground Railroad and had a plan for a hidden room to house the "passengers." That first night, three runaway "passengers" had been led to the Rankin "station." They were fed and hidden on the property. Clarissa was amazed at how they had made their way across the Ohio River and up the one hundred steps of the "freedom stairway" taking them to the Rankin House. She heard firsthand from the conductor what had just happened to another group of escaping slaves four nights before, who had tried to move on a full-moon night and had been captured. This experience at the Rankins' confirmed in Clarissa's heart as well as her father's that they must help. On returning home, the work on the secret room in the basement off the ravine began.

Her father had hired only Quaker builders from another area of Northern Ohio who were sympathetic to the cause, ensuring that no one local would know about the room. Thus, the House of the Four Pillars became a stop on the Underground Railroad.

Journal Entry
November 22ⁿᵈ, 1850
"I met the passenger"

Tonight, my life changed. I didn't know it then but looking back I see how God had arranged my future destiny. God knew my heart and what I needed in this world to make me truly happy. I thought I was happy, but I would soon come to know real happiness.

Tonight, I met "the passenger." I was doing the usual. Our house was a "station" on the Underground Railroad. My father had been the "stationmaster" since 1849 after returning from the Rankin house. Once my father met more of those escaping and heard their stories, he couldn't say no as the Toledo area became a critical layover for slaves escaping to Canada. He was a "stationmaster" until he became too ill to make the trek from the Maumee River through the deep ravine that led to the basement of our house. Then I assumed his "stationmaster" role.

The clear night had been unusually cold with temperatures right at freezing. Clear nights with little moonlight meant safe travel for the "passengers" on the railroad as they "followed the drinking gourd." I had prepared the secret room and made my way down through the ravine wearing all black and a heavy black hooded woolen cape to help hide my movements from any moonlight that might pop through. The night winds suddenly started howling, bringing icy rain pelting my skin, stinging like hundreds of bee stings as I made my way down towards the Maumee. I quickly found the "conductor" alone by a large tree.

"I got some baggage, ma'am. Do you have a place to store it until the next train goes out?"

"Well, I certainly do."

The conductor motioned and three people moved from the dark shadows of the trees along the riverbank. There were two young men and a very elderly, sick woman. They had no coats, gloves, or shoes. I took off my woolen cape to put around the elderly woman's shoulders. She sighed and slumped as she passed out. The young men took turns carrying her as we made our way through the steep, narrow ravine approaching a high hill and our property. Making their way up the steep incline, slippery from the icy rain, caused the young man carrying the elderly lady to slip and almost roll back down. A quick grab from the other man saved them. We stopped to catch our breath, realizing what could have been. Onward we climbed and finally crested the hill, and I could see the candle in the lower window. Making haste, we got inside and bolted the door behind us. I directed them through the false pantry wall laden with canned goods and into the hidden inner chamber where a lantern was burning. A warm, cheery glow was coming from the fireplace along with changes of clothes and shoes. Next came the warm soup and bread, cots, and blankets. Dad had built this space with purpose. He had a flue put in that connected to our main house chimney, eliminating two separate sources of smoke coming from the chimney. I stoked the fireplace embers, bringing them to blazing life. I added a few logs to heat the room and showed them the pile of wood for the night.

Once they were warmed and nourished, the travelers shared their story. They were the sons of the sickly elderly woman, named Abigail. They had risked everything to get their mother free. Abigail had been around on plantations for many years, and the older slave women were valuable commodities to the slave owners because they basically ran the day-to-day activities on the plantations and knew all the workings, dirty laundry, and secrets. They were the ones to raise and train younger slave boys or girls how to do the jobs both inside and outside the house. Most of them had raised the children of their masters and had more influence over the affairs of the plantation than many of the wives.

I helped the sons wrap Abigail in blankets and gave her some warm broth. She rallied enough to smile but after a few more hearty spoons of broth went to sleep. Tomorrow I would check on her and the sons. They would stay a few days until we got notice of a northern conductor's arrival. Then I would take them back to the river where they would leave in the dead of night and move on their next leg to Canada, either by going over Lake Erie or around it through Detroit and crossing the Detroit River.

Journal Entry
November 25th, 1850

With just Dad and me for Thanksgiving, we had so much food left over, I sent our cook home with some for her family before taking the rest of the food to the basement's hidden room and the passengers. They were hungry and ready to eat. We only went to the basement and hidden room after dark. Even though our neighbors were sympathetic, you never knew when slave hunters might be lurking around, ready to pounce. They were ruthless and didn't care if innocent people got hurt in their efforts to return a slave for the reward.

The sons, Sam, and Isaiah regained their strength and were fit for travel. The following night was to be clear and almost moonless. A perfect night for running the underground railroad and a conductor to make a run northward. Abigail was another story. She was still feverish, and her breathing was shallow and congested. She would need more days to get her strength back.

"Tomorrow night would be good for your next travel, but your mom isn't up to it. You can all stay here until she is well enough to travel."

Sam spoke. "Man said we must travel on the 26th. He say winter is coming early and he ain't making promises for more runs to get to Canada after that. We must leave tomorrow night."

"But your mom isn't well! She would likely not survive the

trip. Can't you stay until she gets well? Maybe just a week? Would a week be that much different?"

"No, no ma'am. We gotta try. We've come this far from Tennessee. We gotta go. Momma is strong. She'll make it."

I felt Abigail's head and her fever was still high. Even with warm new clothes and shoes, she would struggle breathing in the cold night traveling conditions. What would happen? I'd pray for a miracle.

Journal Entry
November 26th, 1850

Breaking my own rules right after lunch, I cautiously made my way down to the basement door, which was only visible from the ravine. I had talked to Dad about the situation and we prayed. After praying for some time, he spoke.

"Clarissa, there is only one solution. Those boys have their full life ahead of them. They need to go. Abigail has worked long and hard. She may or may not make it. I want you to offer her the choice to stay here with us and be a free woman of color or to go with her boys. She is welcome to join our family, and we will give her a room, board and a sufficient wage that would allow her to send money to her boys when they reach Canada. She can help with the running of the house as she is able and free up Kathy our current cook and housecleaner. Kathy has been asking for more time off to help her youngest with his schooling and to babysit her first grandchild, who seems to have colic a lot and keeps her daughter from going to work. What do you think?"

I didn't need to think. My heart was full, and this was right. God was making a way if Abigail wanted it. I made my way surreptitiously down the steps and around to the basement back door... I once again prayed that God would help Abigail make the right decision. Even though she was feverish, she was still lucid. I'd see if the fever had broken. If so, she might make it. If not, I would present the offer.

I found Abigail still with fever. It seemed less but she was still hot. I presented the choices. Sam and Isaiah looked stunned and then looked at their mom with tears in their eyes and told her that they wanted her to be a part of their new life and see their children grow. They didn't want to leave her behind.

"Help me sit boys." Abigail mumbled.

The boys jumped up and immediately went to their mother's side, helping her sit up in the bed. Sam sat behind her supporting her back.

"Boys, you know your momma loves you more than life itself. And seein' them free young'uns you will have one day would make me the proudest momma this side of the Mississippi. But I'm not fit for those last legs of the journey. You know we were told those slave hunters know that we gotta cross the big lake or go around it and cross that river and they will be extra a-lookin' for our likes, in the ports or the border towns. If I would be weak and couldn't keep up, and you boys got a-taken back because of me, it would kill me. No sir, you're a-goin' and I'm a-stayin' and I'm mighty thankful to the Lord up above for bringin' us to this station. My journey ends here as a free woman of color. I will be free. Free as I once was as a young girl. Free to do what I want and not be at the beck and call of some master. Besides I'm goin' to send you money when you let me know you arrived safe in Canada."

With that she hugged the boys and asked to lay back down. It was settled. After dinner tonight, the boys would be taking their next rail journey and Abigail was staying. For some reason, this felt right.

Janet shut the journal, laid it on the nightstand and turned off the light. She couldn't wait to read more of the journal and find out what happened and why Clarissa's life had been changed forever. She rolled to her side and went to sleep quickly, dreaming of laughing children, elevators, waltzes, dark eyes, and claret wine. An elusive man in a military cape she had never seen before was searching for her but couldn't find her. His face was a blur.

Chapter 4
A Destiny and a Mask

The Present, Early Morning
Janet's House

Janet awoke, refreshed and hungry, laughing as her belly

rumbled. She felt as she had years ago on a special school day or field trip. She was excited and didn't know why. But she hadn't felt like this in a long time. Maybe she had finally turned the corner from her past on the way to her future. She picked up her phone to see the time. 5:50 AM. *What? I can't believe I feel this energized after reading half the night.* Realizing she was wide awake and not likely to go back to sleep, Janet sighed and decided to make the day a fresh start in her life. She would let go of the past and Liam like scattering ashes in the wind, never to see the remains again.

She tried to picture Liam so she could officially say goodbye, but instead the picture that popped into her mind was of a man with dark, thick, wavy hair, a matching dark, thick moustache, long sideburns, and dark brown eyes that she could drown in. She giggled, wondering where that image had come from. She felt like she must have dreamt of him or seen a picture of him somewhere because he seemed so familiar. There was something about children and searching, but that was all vague now.

She stretched her arms over her head as she sat on the side of the bed and walked around to the trunk. An urgent prompting led her to open the lid and view the items in the daylight to get a better look at the full contents. She lifted the veil gently again and laid it back down on the floor beside the trunk — when her eyes caught the edge of something lying between the trunk and her bed. It was the purest red claret color she had ever seen, and it appeared to be the tip of a ribbon. She laid down the muslin package containing the veil, and with a gentle pull began to ease the ribbon out from its hiding place. As she pulled, an edge of white wool began to peek out as well. *How strange! Where did this come from?* Janet then remembered hearing something fall last night. This must have been it. She gently pulled the claret ribbon and found it was securing a parchment scroll tucked inside the white woolen pouch.

Janet froze. The moment her eyes saw the scroll, it was like electricity had passed between the scroll through the ribbon to her fingers. It was so strong; she dropped the ribbon and rubbed her fingertips. *What the heck? That's impossible. I must be more tired than I thought.*

Janet sighed and took hold of the ribbon again. Nothing happened. "Let's see what this thing is," she muttered to herself.

The mysterious scroll was out far enough that Janet was able to scoop it up in both her hands and stand up. Her body shook as if she had just stepped out of a deep freeze. Her eyes were drawn to the scroll. *What could this thing say? Why do I feel like time has stopped? This is crazy, Janet! Snap out of it.*

Janet took a deep breath to bring her back to some form of normalcy. Why was she feeling confused? *Brain fog. Yes, that's it.* Carrying the woolen pouch with the scroll peeking out, she walked over to the side of the bed and laid it down. Her arms felt like spaghetti. Forcing her hand out to pull the ribbon and finish untying the bow, Janet released the scroll, and it popped open, perfectly flat. *None of this is making sense. Something tied up like this for so long would not want to unroll by itself.* Yet here this scroll lay, perfectly flat. The ink was as dark and vivid as if it had been written today. The parchment was fragile but thick, and for its age was not cracked.

"What do you have to tell me?" Janet spoke out loud as if the scroll was a living thing. Using two tissues, she gently picked up the scroll and began to read out loud.

If You Dare
Wear it if you dare – Wear it and become fair.
Wear it if you suffer – Wear it as your buffer.
Through new eyes you will see – just who God created you to be.
Watch what a new view will do – Transformation into the new you.
Trust the Mask and lose the past.
Life will take on purpose and meaning – The truths of life will reveal
your inner being.
Time and circumstances brought the Mask to your hand –
Wear it and find your special Godly man.
His love will forever be only for you – Trust the Mask and say, "I
do."
Love awaits, make no mistake
The passing of time has brought your season –
To move forward, you must give up logic and reason.

Janet read it again and then a third time. What was it talking about? What did it mean? Was this an omen? Who had written it, and why? Was the Clarissa of the journal the writer? Was there a Mask of some sort in the trunk? The poem certainly had some great promises if they had the power to become true.

Janet laid down the scroll. She felt normal. *Must have been my imagination or something. I guess I am more tired than I thought.*

"Now let's see what's inside this pouch." With the same tissues, Janet carefully opened the pouch and pulled out a very delicate lace item. From her training she knew that it had been tatted or a similar technique. Tatting was a craft some say came from China and some say Ancient Egypt. Small, tiny shuttles, each with a single strand of thread or silk were looped and knotted, creating delicate lace. She had never seen this pattern before. It was so delicate, but it was more solid like a cloth. Janet unfolded it and saw that it was, indeed, a mask. It had two holes for eyes; the nose was made three dimensional so it would fit snug on the face; an elliptical opening formed the mouth. The Mask would fit an average face and was designed with ties to secure around the back of the head.

So, the poem was speaking of a literal mask. How strange. It was like nothing she had encountered in any of her studies and research. It was possible that this was a "one of a kind" mask. The skill that it had taken to create was unbelievable. It had apparently never been worn because it was perfectly clean and the purest white. She knew it had to be at least as old as the wedding dress, which was certainly from the early 1850s.

Janet sat down on the bed beside the pouch and the scroll, laying the Mask gently on top of the white pouch. She picked up the scroll and read through the poem once again. *This must be the Mask of the poem, but I don't understand how putting this thing on can get the love of your life to take notice of you.* She laughed out loud. "Well for sure someone may notice the curiosity of such a mask, but how that would lead to true and lasting love is really a stretch."

Janet laid the scroll down and it continued to stay perfectly flat. *That is such an odd thing!* She shook her head and got up to go through the full contents of the trunk. From the top drawer of her dresser, she retrieved a pair of white cotton gloves. She slipped her hands into them, knowing they would protect the treasures from any oils on her hands.

She inspected the veil first. It was a classic example of the Victorian style. Long, flowing and trailing after the bride. It was made to be secured with tortoise shell combs and when the combs were secured, it caused a pearl, beaded and sequined headband to pop up, creating the effect of a tiara.

The corset and petticoats were all the same era, as were the purse, fan, and parasol. Finally, she opened the muslin that held the wedding dress. She wasn't disappointed. The work was exquisite and delicate. There were pearl beads, ribbons created miniature rosebuds, and layering of silk lace over satin must have been stunning to see on this bride! Janet lifted the dress with its attached crinolines up and out of the trunk. She gently shook out the garments, letting everything settle.

Walking over to the oval mirror, Janet held the dress up to herself for a look. It was exquisite. The standing collar with a V-shaped front connected to a tight-fitting bodice with a small waist. It was made to accentuate the neck. The sleeves were puffy at the shoulders, tapering down tight at the elbow, then once again flaring out to reach to just past the wrist. The skirt flared from the cinched waist with rows of ruffled satin and lace. The rose clusters created by the ribbons and sequins accented the design in the lace. With a corset, she just might fit the dress. She closed her eyes and immediately saw herself wearing the dress to a ball. Enjoying what was playing in her mind, Janet imagined herself walking over to a floor-length wall mirror in a ballroom and looking at herself. Indeed, she had on the dress, but it was the same claret red as the ribbon that had tied the scroll. She saw herself with a mask that resembled large sequined glasses with matching claret feathers adorning the temples. She giggled and it brought her back to reality and her bedroom. The oval mirror showed Janet holding just the yellowed wedding dress. *Strange visions in my head. This trunk, journal, clothing, and mask have seemed to create in me a whimsical "what if" that needs to be checked back to reality.*

Her cell phone rang, jolting her back to 2022. Gently laying the dress down on the bed, Janet went to her bedstand and snatched up the phone. "Hello, Janet speaking." The number that had come up was a familiar one in London: the Victoria and Albert Museum, her new employer.

"Janet, this is Vickey. I hope I didn't wake you. I'm on my lunch hour and wanted to connect to see if you can arrange your plans to start your new job early. We felt we needed to get the invites out several weeks sooner than originally planned, and since that is part of your new position, we could use you here ASAP."

"Well…what is sooner?"

"Could you come by the end of the week?"

"You mean in five to seven days?" Janet's voice went up an octave.

"Yes, well I know it's sudden, especially since you thought you had another three weeks, but Marketing and Sales wants to get the publicity out and drop hints of some of those attending. Hopefully the press will begin to give us some free coverage and start the tongues wagging. They think that it will create a run on the ticket sales, so the event becomes the prized social gathering of the season. If anyone is notoriety, then our event will be the must-have ticket, with the must-be-seen dress, and have the winning bids at auction."

"Well, I suppose I can pull it off. My parents are going to manage renting my place for me and taking care of the oversight while I'm gone. It just means they will have to get out the rental notice ASAP. I've already boxed up my personal stuff and put it in storage. So, it's just getting my clothing packed, notifying the utilities, and turning over the keys to Mom and Dad."

"Great! See you soon. Send me an email with your flight info and we will have a service pick you up and take you to your new apartment. It has been cleaned and painted. It comes furnished, and a bunch of us took care of some dishes, bedding, towels, etc. You can decorate and get what you want later. I'll make sure that there is coffee, I know you Americans are coffee lovers and don't do tea, but I did put some tea bags in the cabinet too. I'll pick up some fruit, milk, bread, and cheese. That should cover until you can get to the grocery."

"Thanks Vickie! I really appreciate it. As soon as we hang up, I'll get things rolling for the move."

Chapter 5
Donning the Mask

New Year's Eve, 1850
*House of Four Pillars**
Toledo Area, Ohio

I hated parties. They were always full of women and men, vying for each other's attention in hopes to find the best match to secure their future. I had no such need for that type of entertainment. My life was happy, fulfilled by caring for the passengers who were more frequent now. The family business was going strong and financially our money was well invested. Occasionally there would be a rumor of growing tensions between those who wanted to see slavery ended and those who saw it as their right to make a profit and establish enterprises or empires. A war or even skirmishes could bring a downward turn in the economy, or it could have the opposite effect, depending upon the business and economic perspective. Regardless, I felt assured that our financial future was secure.

Tonight, I feared that all my worries and dread would be experienced at the ball. Father had made me promise to attend a New Year's Eve masquerade ball that was a fundraiser to update and expand the Lucas County Orphan Asylum, because the number of orphans had grown so great since 1830. A new wing was needed that included a medical ward staffed with rotating doctors from the Toledo Medical Association. Many orphans came with malaria, cholera or typhoid fever that had killed their family. Although the "Black Swamp" was now drained, many outlying areas still had epidemics that even wiped-out entire villages. My own father almost died years ago and continued to have reoccurring bouts with it.

There would be a silent auction at the ball, and Father had donated the use of a private railroad car for up to six months to the highest bidder. The minimum bid was $1,000. The car was opulently furnished, could sleep six and accommodate twelve in the lounge. It came complete with attendants plus all food and drinks. It was expected to draw many high bids.

While I was getting dressed for the ball, Abigail came and shared with me for the first time about the Mask. She wanted me to wear the Mask for the ball. I sat and listened to her farfetched story about a mask of special powers that went back to the Queen of Sheba and King Solomon. She shared how through the tribal lines the Mask had been passed down and how every one of those who received the Mask and took the chance to wear it had their destiny changed. I listened with a skeptical mind. Reading my facial expressions, she laughed and let me read the poem. I laughed even more once I read the poem out loud.

"Abigail!" I teased. "Do you really believe this? It just seems too much like a fairytale."

"No, Miss Clarissa, I'm a-swearin' it's true. I was the one to receive

it from my tribal line which goes back to the Queen. I ain't lyin' Miss. I put it on, and the Lord be true and strike me dead, it changed me. The eldest son of our rival tribe, Efosa, was out huntin' and happened to come across me washin' out some dirty clothes in the stream. He'd seen me many times before and always snickered at me like I was a lowly runt. But when I looked up at him with the Mask on, I'm swearin', his eyes got big, and he became short of breath. He yelled across the stream at me and told me, 'You're mine. Don't you go off and hide. I'm comin' for you and have twenty head of cattle and twelve goats for your father.' I was shocked because he was s'possed to marry one of his own, but now when he seen me, he said that and ran off toward his village. I was glad, because I had always looked upon him with want'n eyes."

Now I really laughed. "That great of a change huh?"

"No, Miss, you don't see. You don't know and understand the power of the Mask. I knew. I had seen the change in my face and the way that I appeared in the reflection of the stream. I could feel the difference. I felt full and alive with hope and desire for more in life. When I looked and saw what I had become and how I felt inside about my future, I knew it was true. You put it on, and you will see it and feel it too."

"Abigail, I have no problem believing that you might have been a beautiful woman in your prime. But if what you say is true, why are you here? How did you end up a slave and not married to your Efosa or someone as the poem says who would love you and you would be living a happy life?"

"They came, Miss, they came!"

"Who came, Abigail?"

"The slave men. They came with guns and dogs and whips. They raided the village of Efosa first and took everyone by surprise. No one escaped. The ones that they didn't shoot were put on a ship, in chains. Efosa fought back and was killed. Two of our tribe were out fishing at the falls and heard the gunshots. They were able to see the destroyed and burned village from the cliff at the top of the falls. They hurried back and told us. We all scattered in the jungle to hide. I knew, Miss, that if I kept the Mask on, I would be raped before I ever got to the ships. So, I took off the Mask and rolled up the scroll and put all inside the pouch. I grabbed one of the babies of my sister and stuffed the pouch in the material I wrapped the baby in and prayed to the good Lord that the men would be blind and not see it. Without the Mask, I wasn't a looker. They found me in the cave because the baby needed milk, and I didn't have any to give it, so they heard the baby and found us. They whipped me on the legs, and I

feared for the baby and the Mask. But they didn't take the baby from me but just dragged me with the baby and all the others they had found to the ships. We were all separated on the ships so that no one could be with family. They had people from many villages on the ships."

"How did you feed the baby? Did it die on the trip?"

"No Miss, another woman in the belly of the ship had a newborn that died in their village raid. Praise the Lord Almighty, she took one look at the baby and at me and knew. She latched onto the baby and took care of him from that point on. She became his momma. I removed the Mask pouch and used the wrap from the baby to stuff under my dress. It made me look with child and so the horrible slave men left me alone, unlike the other girls. The Mask protected me, kept me safe and traveled, by God's help, with me all this time."

"Abigail, you mean that since that day, you have never had the Mask on again or seen any of your family or tribe?"

"Yes, Miss. My heart breaks every day for my family. The life I had from that moment on wasn't the life to put on the Mask. I became a different person, but not the person who had a destiny with the Mask. The slave traders changed all of that. Once in America, at first, I was moved around and owned by several owners. Moving around kept them from raping me. Then I came to the plantation where I finally stayed. I had to say I lost the baby, and I sewed the pouch into my clothes. No one ever knew it was hidden in my clothes. I had my two sons, because the owner forced me to give myself to one of his slaves to raise up more slaves. I didn't have a daughter, for which I thank the good Lord."

"Oh, I'm so sorry, Abigail, for all that you have gone through. You must be very sad to not have a daughter to pass the Mask to."

"No Miss, I ain't sad. I'm very happy. The life she would grow up into would not have been made better by the Mask. No, she would have had a life of being the sexual toy of many men. I'm thankful for no daughter. I've got two good boys and I'm thankful for them and that they will with the good Lord's help reach their freedom in Canada soon. God led us here, and now I have a good life with you and your father. I'm soon to be a free person and I can die now in peace once I hear from my boys and know that the Mask is in good hands. Your hands, Miss. That's why you must take it. I know God brought us here and I know deep in my knower that you are to be the one to carry on the legacy of the Mask."

I didn't know what to say. My heart was a tumbled swirl of emotions. In my heart I knew that even as free men in Canada, making a good living and raising up sons and daughters that would have equality was not going to be a quick process for Abigail's sons. I stalled a minute by asking her a question.

"Abigail, I really do believe what you are saying could have happened and ..."

"No, Miss, it really did happen as I've said. The story has been written down and passed onto each designated one and it hasn't possibly happened, it really did happen."

"All right, it really happened to the women in your tribe down through the ages, but how did the poem get into English? I'm sure whoever wrote the poem in the first place wrote it in your tribal language. But what you showed me was in English. How did that happen?"

"Well Miss, my tribe is from what is known as Ethiopia or Abyssinia. Our country has been around for at least a thousand or more years. We are older than Egypt. But the Queen of Sheba was born from one Ethiopian parent and the other from Saba or Yemen. She was heir to both countries. She divided her time and responsibilities between Ethiopia and Yemen, expanding their exports to both the East and Mediterranean areas. Both of her countries were traders of spices, incense like frankincense, gemstones and animal skins, cloth, equipment, weapons, and cattle. Our tribe was known for our fair skin and beauty and the production of fine cloth. About a hundred years ago, a merchant from Ragusa, Italy, came to our village to buy and sell. He was a believer in our God, he said, and knew about the legend of the Mask. He had heard that we followed the God of King Solomon. The Queen had seen firsthand the reality of King Solomon's God and saw how God watched over all that the King set his hand to do. The Queen returned with her son after several years to make sure her two countries were still strong and safe. The Queen taught her people to believe in the Hebrew God and to forsake the other gods like the nations around us."

Abigail continued, "This trader spoke many tongues, and could read Hebrew, the languages of Yemen, Ethiopia, Egypt, Spain, and the British Isles. He was there to trade but he also wanted to see the legendary mask and how it made all the women beautiful who wore it. We knew he wanted to get his hands on it and sell it. So, we told him that it had deteriorated years ago and all that was left was the scroll. The chief agreed to let him see the scroll if the merchant would translate it into all the languages that he knew, but he had to do so in the sight of the chief. As a greater incentive, the chief would give him a jar of prized incense and the skin of a rare white lion upon completion.

"The original scroll and the copies in the pouch had been passed to

me and it was my sacred duty to protect them, and I did. When I landed in America, I knew that English was going to be the only language going forward that would be needed. I wasn't going to get back to my village. Even if I did one day make it back, my tribe was gone. Life would never follow the same path again for the Mask or for me. The others I burned, except for the original. I still have it. Do you want to see it too?"

"No Abigail, you hold it since that is the last of your connection to your past life. I am just so overwhelmed when I think about all of this. I'm amazed and I'm sad all at the same time."

"Miss, the happiest thing other than my boys' safety in Canada is that the Mask lives on, giving hope and love and a future full of potential and destiny to the one God has directed. As, I said, I believe that person is you. Just try on the Mask and see what happens, Miss. If you don't see or feel a change both in and out, I won't ask you to take it. I will find another owner. But Miss, I know you will be the owner. I just know."

How could I say no to just try it on? Surely a piece of cloth as she had described it could not really make that kind of difference. I got dressed and Abigail hooked the closures up the back of the gown. I had picked out a claret-red gown with the intent of reusing it again either for a Valentine's dinner or with some updates, next Christmas. Stylish clothing and society galas were not high on my list of priorities.

Abigail brought in the Mask from her quarters and opened the muslin that wrapped the pouch. I was amazed at the purity of the white wool.

"Abigail, how did you keep it so white and clean all those years of hiding it in your clothing? I'm astonished at how beautiful the pouch still is."

"Miss, it just stays this way. I da know. Many a time it got soaked as I labored out in the rain or had my clothing caked with mud from the fields. It just stays white."

Now I was even more curious about the contents of the pouch.

"Here, Miss."

Abigail gently took out the Mask. It looked tatted of silk. As she lifted it up, the Mask tumbled open, revealing a full mask that would cover from the hairline down to the chin. It had ties to keep it in place around the head. I was fascinated how the creator had crafted the contours for the nose, cheekbones, and chin and, there were perfect openings for the eyes and lips.

"Miss, sit down at the mirror and let me help you put it on. Close your eyes."

I closed my eyes and felt Abigail lay the Mask upon my face and tie it in back, fluffing my hair out over the string ties. I was about to open my eyes to see what this tatted mask looked like on my face, but Abigail spoke.

"Keep your eyes closed for a few minutes and just let the Mask and your face become one. If you are the one, the Mask will know and do its work."

What a strange thing to say, "Let the Mask and your face become one and if you are the one, the Mask will know and do its work." I obeyed to give Abigail the understanding that I was giving it my full effort, especially for her understanding when the Mask didn't work, and I gently declined the offer later.

Warmth was the first sensation. But the warmth was followed with the sensation of water touching dry and thirsty skin. It felt wonderful and I found myself letting out a deep sigh.

"Oh Miss! It is working! I knew you were the right one. Open your eyes and look at what is happening."

I opened my eyes to see the last few areas of the Mask disappear upon my face. I was bewildered at what I was seeing and feeling. My skin had absorbed the tatted Mask completely. I ran my fingers over my face and the Mask was gone to both sight and the touch of my fingers. Yet, I could feel it resting against my skin. My fingers went to my hair, and I lifted it up and then ran a comb through my hair and the comb never snagged the ties. Yet I could feel the tension from them that held the Mask on my face. I leaned in closer to the mirror and brought the whale oil lamp close. The Mask was just gone. No hint of an edge around my lips, hair line or eyes. Yet I could feel the Mask still in place.

"I know, Miss. That's the miracle. On the right person, it disappears. No one will ever know that you are wearing the Mask. Now Miss, sit back and take a good look at your face and hair. Just like I saw my changes in the river that day, you will see it too."

I leaned back like she said and really looked for the first time at my reflection and not the intricacies of trying to find the Mask. I was the same but different. I was better or enhanced somehow. My hair was thicker in appearance and when I ran my fingers through, it felt thicker, with just the hint of curl. Not too much, just a subtle hint that added a perky bounce. My face was also the same but improved. The dark circles under my eyes from the short nights with passengers coming and going were gone. My cheeks and skin had a glow like I had on the costliest Parisian cosmetics. My cheeks felt firmer. My lips were a little poutier and appeared to have rouge, but I hadn't applied any. My eyes seemed to have become a darker and more intense blue. I was me, but a better me.

Abigail knew from my eyes that I saw the changes. She smiled into the mirror at me.

"Yes, Miss, it's true. It's you but better. The Mask takes all your attributes and heightens them with your inner beauty of heart. Your inner light shines through. Now Miss, stand up and look at the rest of you. Take a deep breath and think about how you feel about yourself and life and your future."

As I stood, my muscles felt stronger, my legs, tired from the steep incline from the ravine, felt fit and lean. I swore my waist was a little smaller and my bosom was fuller. I took a deep breath, letting it out slowly. Did I feel different? Yes, I did. I couldn't put my finger on the reason, but I felt more alive. It was like a deep peace and satisfaction had come over me. I felt relaxed and the dread of going to the New Year's Eve ball was gone. I felt a kind of expectation almost like a child on Christmas Eve, wondering what I was going to find the next day.

"Abigail, I don't understand. How does this all work? It is impossible in the natural."

"Yes Miss, but it's the power of the Mask for miracles. Legend passed down with the Mask said that King Solomon had been given it as a gift for his wise counsel that saved another king of the East's kingdom. As a thank you, the Mask was made for King Solomon to give to a worthy bride. When the Queen of Sheba came and contended with Solomon to solve her riddles and later accepted the God of Israel, Solomon saw in her a wife worthy of the Mask. The Queen of Sheba was given the mask to wear on their wedding day and she wore it from that moment on until her death. It was then passed down to the first daughter of their son Ben Sira, who found a bride and passed it down to their daughter until it reached me. I am giving it to you, Miss. It has shown that it has chosen you by blending and becoming one with you. If you wear it, what the poem said will come true. You will find the man just right for you for a lasting love. So, are you going to wear it to the ball tonight? If you are, you will need this."

Abigail brought out of her pocket a perfectly matching claret half mask with matching feathers and a wand to hold the mask with over my eyes.

"Now sit back down and let me fix your hair with the claret ribbon from the poem. It will work perfect to pull up your hair on this side, just exposing enough of the curve of your neck to entice a look and may catch the eye of your true love."

"Abigail, I know that this Mask is very unusual, but finding my true love tonight at the ball would be a miracle, since I'm not looking and have quite decided that being single is just fine. Besides, I have seen all the

eligible bachelors from here and I can tell you, I wouldn't walk down the aisle with any of them."

Abigail smiled knowingly. "Sure, Miss, I understand."

Chapter 6
Relocation & Reallocation

Present, A Week Later, Early Afternoon
London Apartment

Janet directed where she wanted all her bags and the trunk to go. She also paid an oversize fee to have the trunk with the wedding dress and clothing shipped to her in London. Her parents asked why she would take the trunk and pay such a premium fee to do so. Janet couldn't give them a logical response — she just felt like she couldn't separate herself from the trunk and its contents. She used the extra space in the trunk for some of her own things as justification, but carried the pouch and poem in her carry-on. She read the journal on the trans-Atlantic flight and couldn't wait to discover what happened with Clarissa at the New Year's Eve Ball. As she closed the journal in preparation for landing at London/Heathrow, Janet giggled at the coincidence that both she and Clarissa had New Year's Eve galas in their lives.

The trunk was placed at the foot of her bed in the new apartment. It had taken two men to carry it up the flight of stairs to her floor. She didn't have room to bring the oval mirror — it was stored in her parents' garage for now. Janet's new work mates were coming by in about an hour to take her to dinner and to help her get the lay of the land for markets, restaurants, and the Tube routes to work. Tomorrow, she would be in her new job working on the guest list for the New Year's Eve ball. But tonight, after the tour, she would read what happened at Clarissa's New Year's Eve ball. Would the Mask really bring her true love?

Present 10:30 pm
London Apartment

Janet finished the last of her unpacking, took a shower and crawled into bed, tired and curious about the journal. She set her alarm for 6 AM and snuggled down to read. *Will Clarissa really meet the love of her life like Abigail and the poem claimed? This journal is just like a romance novel. I can't believe something like this can happen in reality. But it makes for a good read and a great legend for a display in the museum. If nothing else, the tatted mask will be a unique addition.*

Journal Entry
Late New Year's Eve, 1850

It happened. I can't believe it. Everything that Abigail said would happen, happened! I believe that my Mr. Right, the potential love of my life, a possible forever love, waltzed literally into my arms last night.

I had let Abigail fix my hair and it did look enchanting. The claret mask was really a mask made for teasing and flirting. The idea of flirting began bubbling inside of me and took me by surprise. A part of my personality that had taken a back seat for years was now awakening.

I arrived stylishly late to the ball. The music was lively, and the hall was full. The candles and oil lights made a magical glow to the rooms. The eligible single people were strolling, mingling, conversing in small groups, and dancing. The older men were in corners with heads bent, arguing politics about the growing tensions over slavery, or were coming and going for drinks in the gentlemen's rooms.

The married women or the older spinsters were sitting in short rows of chairs arranged in semicircles, and animatedly conversing about children, fashion, and the latest gossip. I would have planted myself in the middle of one of those circles on other occasions, but I had donned the Mask, biding my time until I could leave and end the tedious dialogs. I rather longed to be conversing with the men on the politics and rumors of the growing tensions in the South and in Washington. But women were not welcomed into the men's circle. Having helped many passengers on the Underground Railroad, I had seen and heard firsthand the stories of abuse and enslavement. I could tell them all a thing or two. Not to mention, I could keep up with any financial talk because running the family business made me very informed and cognizant.

But tonight, I was feeling like taking the risk to see if the men could handle a woman barging into their world, keeping up in the conversation, and having strong opinions to voice. I glanced at the various groups and chose one made up exclusively of men, who were partners with our family businesses as well as some who were in politics.

As I sauntered up to the group, all conversation ceased, and the men with their backs to me turned. All the men's eyes were on me. I felt their stares and would have been uncomfortable before tonight. But tonight, I was more alive and confident than ever.

"Hello gentlemen, mind if I join you? I am dying for good conversation. What say you about the current tensions over slavery?"

Silence fell for what felt like an eternity. Then one of our business partners spoke up.

"Well, might I say Miss Clarissa, that you look stunning tonight? You must let my wife know what new boutique products you are using."

"Well thank you, Mr. Folsom. I will be happy to do that. So do tell, you just got back from visiting in Washington, DC, and I'm sure you heard how the current tensions are running." I wasn't about to let them off the hook by changing the topic in hopes I would go away.

Sensing that I was not going to be put off, he cleared his throat and continued. "Indeed, Miss. The tones of conversations have become more heated and more frequent about what's to be done. Many groups are trying to introduce legislation to abolish slavery. But the palms of many influential politicians and businessmen are greased by the tobacco, cotton, and peanut industries."

"Well gentlemen, I do hope that there would be enough Christian morals to tackle the greed of…" But I didn't get the rest out — a deep voice close behind me interrupted.

"Excuse me, ma'am, but I just love this waltz and would like you to partner with me for it."

The voice caused every hair on my arms and up my neck to stand on end. The men's attention turned to the deep, strong voice. I was about to tell this man I didn't appreciate the interruption and no I wasn't interested in this waltz. I spun around — he was standing closer than I expected. His presence overwhelmed me. Shying away, I lost my balance — but he caught me in his strong arms, his hands on my waist steadied me, keeping me from toppling over my own feet. I looked up to feign protest, but his gaze was strong and burned into my eyes. I had to look away quickly because all breath left my lungs. I started to swoon and hated myself for reacting this way. The unknown gentlemen had made me lightheaded and every sane thought, sharp comeback, and witty retort, fled somewhere into obscure crannies in my mind.

"Oh, I'm sorry…" His deep voice was like thick, warm honey pouring over me and soaking into my heart. In a low, soft voice, he whispered for my ears only, "I shouldn't have stepped so close to you, but I must admit, your scent and the curve of your neck revealed by the way your hair is *pulled up enticed me. I needed a closer look. I do apologize. It was very ungentlemanlike." As he spoke, he let go of my waist and bowed. "Do forgive me."*

I couldn't speak. I could barely breathe. I just stared at the most handsome face and attractive physique of any man I had met or even seen. But this man was not from this area of Ohio. I would have surely seen him at one of my business meetings. How did he get invited?

"Allow me to introduce myself, since I so boldly interrupted your conversation. But it looks like the group you were talking to has left for drinks in the men's quarters. I'm Charles Adams Gillmore, from the Black River area near Elyria. And who do I have the honor of addressing?"

I must say, for someone who always has a quick response, I was tongue-tied and breathless. What was it about this man? I just wanted to be held by him with those strong arms. I cleared my throat.

"Clarissa Toupes," I managed to squeak out. But I regained my voice quickly. "Yes, it was rude of you to interrupt like you did, but seeing that the gentlemen have retired to their lounge for drinks, I say you do owe me two waltzes, sir."

Where had that come from? Charles laughed with deep pleasure.

"Yes ma'am, and so you shall have them."

He offered his arm, and off we went onto the dance floor. From that point on we danced every dance until the ball ended. He asked if he could escort me home, and I was delighted. I didn't want to part from his company. At the door, I thought for sure he was going to kiss me, and I wouldn't have stopped him. But instead, he took my hand and kissed it.

"Tonight, has been the most remarkable and pleasurable night of my life, Miss Toupes. I have never met anyone like you. You can hold your own with every conversation. You are knowledgeable — unlike so many women. You know your mind and you are not afraid to speak it. I find you fascinating, entertaining and the most beautiful woman I have ever met. I would like to see you again and get to know you more. May I call again tomorrow afternoon…say around 2 PM?"

"Why yes you may, Mr. Gillmore. I would certainly enjoy getting to know you."

"Then until tomorrow. May I call you Clarissa?"

"Yes, if I may call you Charles."

He smiled and my knees went weak. He reached out to take my arm to steady me and then reached across me to open the door. I could smell his cologne — it mingled with the musky perspiration from a night of dancing. The warmth of his body permeated the air even though there was a slight chilly breeze on that mild winter evening.

It took all my strength to step up into the house. Holding onto the door frame, I smiled and said, "I look forward to seeing you tomorrow, Charles."

He smiled, and I was glad that I had hold of the door frame. He turned sharply and headed to his coach. Tomorrow couldn't come soon enough.

Abigail was waiting. She took one look at me and knew. "You met him, didn't you! I knew it, Miss, I just knew you would. That's what the Mask does. It works its miracles to bring you the love of your life and a future that is long and prosperous. I'm assuming he feels the same?"

"I think so, Abigail. We spent the entire evening together. When he brought me home, I didn't want the night to end, and I don't think he did either. He was such a gentleman! There was a part of me that just wanted to be with him forever. He is coming over tomorrow at 2 PM. I don't know if I can get to sleep tonight. I'm giddy like a schoolgirl over her first crush."

"Here, Miss, let's get you out of this gown and I'll draw you a warm bath and make some hot cocoa."

"That sounds marvelous, Abigail. But you will have to help me take off the Mask, so I don't get it wet."

"No Miss, you will not take it off ever again until the love of your life dies, or you pass it to your daughter when she comes of age to marry. It will be your secret."

Now that took a lot to wrap my mind around. But everything that Abigail had told me about the Mask had come true. I believed this part too.

Journal Entry
New Year's Day Evening, 1851

Charles was as punctual as he was handsome. Perfect. He had come looking freshly shaven and smelling masculine with a hint of spice. We talked non-stop about every subject. At the striking of the clock at 5, we laughed when we both asked at the same time if the other was hungry. We looked longingly at each other. Charles smiled and I blushed. It seemed we were hungry for many things.

Father came home from a business trip, and I introduced him to Charles. They went off to talk as I supervised the preparation of dinner. Abigail and our cook shooed me out of the kitchen and told me to get some fresh air because my cheeks were so rosy. Getting some air only brought my thoughts sharper to Charles. I had never felt this way about a man, and to feel it so quickly was unsettling. Everything was happening so fast, too fast to believe. I had read about romance novels spouting fantasies of getting swept off one's feet, but that had been fiction on paper. Now I knew the possibility was real. Charles had me totally captivated and my heart seemed bound to him eternally.

Dinner went well. Father really enjoyed Charles and they laughed and bantered about business, the politics of slavery and the future of America if the tensions over slavery continued to grow. I could tell that my father was getting a feel for what Charles stood for. After dinner, Father asked to speak to me privately, which I thought was very out of the ordinary. I really wanted to ask him if it could wait until the next day, because I didn't want to lose any time away from Charles. But, I agreed because it was so unusual for Father to ask.

"Clarissa, I have to say I am very impressed with Charles. He is finishing up at West Point and has his degree in engineering. He comes from a well-off family and his views are very much aligned with ours. But you also need to know that he has asked for your hand in marriage."

I heard his words, but at the word "marriage," my heart was leaping and wanted to burst out of my chest. I giggled like a kid in a candy shop.

"It seems so unusual with only the two of you meeting just last night. But he said that he had been praying for the right woman that God had for him and he had a dream of seeing her in a red claret ball gown with a matching ribbon in her hair. He had been invited to the ball fundraiser and came out of respect for the business friend who asked him. He didn't expect to stay long, but when he walked into the ball and saw the back of you as the woman in his dream, he knew that God had divinely appointed the meeting."

In my mind all I could think was…The Mask! The Mask! It was all the working of the Mask!

"Father, are you saying that you said yes?"

"No, I told him that you are your own woman, and that I appreciated him asking me for the respect that it shows, but that you must be the one to say yes to the proposal. So will you say yes?"

*Without hesitation I blurted out, "**Yes**! I will say yes, because I too, feel that God has put us together and that even though we have only known each other less that twenty-four hours, I know that this is right. I am destined to marry him."*

"All right, then." He kissed my forehead. "I'm happy to see my girl happy and I can see it in your eyes and the way you look at him. He completes you, doesn't he?"

"Yes, Father. I love him too."

Father said his goodnight, shook Charles's hand and went up to bed. Charles entered the parlor, looking very serious. It was a new expression I had yet to see on him.

"Clarissa, I know that your father has told you of my intentions. But I want you to know that no other woman has ever captivated my heart like you. I love you more than life and I will be your devoted and loving husband all the days of my life if you would, if you could love me too and consent to be my wife."

"Oh Charles, I want nothing more than to be loved by you for as long as God has for us."

At that, Charles advanced toward me, but I ran into his arms, and we kissed a long and passionate kiss. He slowly pulled back and smiled. "You know that with this passion burning between us, we must be married sooner than later. I don't want to wait very long."

Smiling up at him, I knew that he felt the passion inside of me too. So, with the new-found stirrings that the Mask had brought, I looked up at him and said, "Charles Gillmore, will you marry me on February 14th?"

He laughed and picked me up, swinging me off my feet and pulled me close, kissing my face. "Clarissa, you are a forward lady, but I love you and can handle that. Yes! Clarissa, I will marry you on February 14th and not a day later."

Chapter 7
The Setup

The Present, 2:00 AM
London Apartment

Janet closed the journal. She had tears in her eyes. What a story. Could it really have happened that suddenly…that easily, romantically, and passionately? She yawned a deep yawn and laid the journal on the nightstand. There were only a few more entries. Could a life be dramatically altered by something like this historical Mask? Logic and reason told Janet it was only a fantastical, beautiful, whimsical story. But the part of her that was still a secret romantic hoped that such a love could exist.

Turning out the light, Janet rolled onto her side and hugged her other pillow. She needed to get some sleep because morning was coming quickly. She fell asleep almost instantly but dreamed all night of a flowing claret ball gown, a military cape, laughing children and a tall, dark-haired man who was searching for her, and when he found her swept her off her feet.

December 1ˢᵗ
London
The Victoria and Albert Museum

Janet settled into her new job easily. Her office was in the behind-the-scenes rooms where garments and personal articles were cataloged, cleaned, restored, and stored until they had a permanent place for display. Janet loved not being on the business floor. Down there was where the real activities took place. All the plans for the new wing were moving along, and the ones for the New Year's Eve fundraiser ball for the new wing were finished. It was just a matter of recording the RSVPs.

Amid all this activity, Janet thought about Clarissa and Charles and their story in the journal. She had finally finished reading the journal, and the story was really a "happily-ever-after" story. Every time she thought of them, a sparkle came into her life, bringing a momentary tiny firework. What an adventure the two of them must have had. Clarissa hadn't revealed in the journal any of the steamy intimate times, but from her entries, there were many hints of such times. Yet the greatest pleasures she talked about came from how their mundane daily life together just brought them both the deepest of satisfaction. Physical intimacy was apparently the icing on the delicious cake. Even the war and the trials that it brought seemed to bring them closer together as one.

Janet had the wedding dress and other garments thoroughly cleaned within a few weeks of her arrival, in preparation for her donation. One day on a whim she had tried them all on and found they fit as if they had been made for her. The corset took some work to get cinched up, but she managed, and with it the wedding dress fit perfectly. With the right heeled shoes, the dress length would work if she ever wore it. For a moment, the thought of that caused something to stir within her. But there wasn't a reason to wear it and she would contribute it and the Mask to the new Victoria and Albert Museum after the ball.

Janet pushed all fanciful thoughts from her mind as an intern entered her office, bringing more mail full of RSVPs. Janet opened them and began to log who was responding with regrets and who was attending, along with the total number in their party.

Regrets were few. The numbers determined the food count, table setup, people placements for the best conversations and enjoyment, as well as the "who's who" for the press releases. Today's response was the largest so far, with 135 acceptances. At this rate, they might need to add a few more tables. Janet had already planned for this contingency.

Mr. and Mrs. Albert Finch

Mr. and Mrs. Harold Kessler

Mrs. Olivia Myles and companion – Sir John Ross

Janet methodically typed the running list to be able to share the growing numbers and names with the other staff. She reached the last envelope and pulled out the RSVP to extract the name, contact information, food allergies and other specifications from the form.

Sir Richard Alexander Petrovich. A single. That was going to take some rearranging of the tables. Most tables were filled with couples or singles with companions. But an odd number of singles required some creative placement. Janet kept focusing on the name. A part of her thought the name was familiar. It just seemed like she should know him. But her logic didn't agree.

"Where should I put you, Sir Richard Alexander Petrovich?"

"Well—place him wisely." Vickey's voice flowed into the room as she approached Janet's desk. "He is a generous philanthropist. An eligible bachelor, so I hear. The fact that he is attending means that he has a serious interest in this new project. He never usually comes in person, so his presence is noteworthy. But he is also a very humble and unassuming man. If you met him out on the street, you would never know that he was so wealthy. He mingles with the common people; he does his own occasional shopping, I'm told, and loves Victorian history."

"Well then, I best find a good table to place him."

"Actually, that is why I came down here. I heard through the grapevine that he was attending. I think he should be placed at your table."

"*My* table!? Vickey, you can't be serious. I'm not a person who mingles with the aristocrats. I wouldn't know one wine from another or have stories about the vacation spots of Europe."

"Well, everyone loves you here and you are the most versed in the exhibits for the new wing. You can talk about the wing architecture, the budget items, the procured exhibits that we have and those that we are hoping to negotiate for. You're trained in the field, and you know historic clothing from this period. I'd say you could answer any question that is asked."

"Vickey, I don't want to cost you a large charitable donation."

"All the more reason to get your gown picked out and impress. You are the perfect person for him to meet. I'm sure you will do just fine in the conversation and bring honor to the museum and entertain Mr. Petrovich."

Janet wanted to tell Vickey so many other reasons why this wasn't going to be a good idea. Before she could get anything out, Vickey continued.

"Glad that's settled. Let the press know in small increments who are the 'who's who' coming. We need all the free press we can get. There are still a few fish I'm hoping will bite and who won't want to miss the party of the year and getting their pictures in the headlines for attending."

Janet knew it was hopeless. Mr. Richard Alexander Petrovich would be sitting at her table, and she had nothing to wear. She really needed to go shopping.

December 15th
Janet's Apartment

Work had increased in the two weeks since she had to accept that Mr. Richard Alexander Petrovich was going to be at her table. She had written his name down on the seating chart for the table placements and the name tag list and moved on. Now in sixteen days, she needed a ball gown fitting the Victorian Period to show Mr. Petrovich she knew her stuff.

Janet sighed and plopped herself down on the edge of the bed, tired and ready to call it a night. The engravers of the Victorian programs, name tags and seating placement cards were not sure they could get enough card stock and paper to take care of the capacity attendance. The original numbers Vickey had given them before Janet's arrival were too low. *Perhaps I was a little too good with the planning of this event. Now I must make sure it gets solved. A* thought popped into her mind. *Use two different shades of the antique-*

looking card stock. Use one shade for the "Alberts" and one shade for the "Victorias."

Now where did that idea come from? Janet giggled. *I don't know, but I'll take it. It's perfect and will add to the distinguishing of the two personalities — Albert and Victoria.*

Janet turned out the light and rolled into bed. Pulling the covers, she quickly covered her eyes with the duvet because the room wasn't as dark as usual. *Apparently, the moon must be bright tonight,* she thought. Little did she know that the light was the glow from the trunk's keyhole. The Mask was at work.

Friday, December 16th
Janet's Apartment

Janet was awake before the alarm went off, surprised how good she felt even though she had gone to bed late. *I've got to make it a priority to get a dress. Time is running out.* She was thinking of where she might find a vintage dress when her cell rang. Sitting up on the edge of her bed, she grabbed her phone. "Janet speaking."

"This is Vickey. I know it's early, but I needed to know if you have your ball gown yet. I don't want to worry you, but I just talked to some of the ladies who do seamstress jobs on the side, and they said that there isn't a Victorian dress to be found in England. It seems that all those with money and who could afford to go vintage have bought up everything and are having them altered and enhanced to outshine each other. Others hired creation copies of gowns that will be in the new exhibition. It is causing a press feeding frenzy and we are getting news agents from Europe and even as far as the Mediterranean, letting us know they are coming for the red-carpet entrance of all those in attendance. I've been told that you can't find a hotel room for the event."

Janet's heart sank and she felt suddenly sick to her stomach. No dress was possible. What was she to do?

"Janet are you there?"

"Yes Vickey, don't worry, I've got it all under control." It was a bold-faced lie, but she just wanted to get off the phone and cry or throw up.

"Good, I knew that you would. You have done such a perfect job of turning this event into a mega showcase that will generate all the funds and maybe more than we need. Wouldn't that be wonderful? We'll have the means to procure even more, thanks to you. Hey, I gotta run, I'm doing an interview with a major American broadcaster. Why don't you take the day off and just enjoy a leisurely day as a little 'thank you' for all the hard work you have put into this event? I'll see you back in the office on Monday."

Janet hung up the call, fell back on the bed and fought back the tears. Why had she waited? Now she wasn't going to be wearing anything vintage. Not only would she lose the Petrovich monies, but her job was probably going to be at stake because she had just told an outright lie to her boss.

Janet closed her eyes. An immediate vision of herself in a claret red ball gown danced and swirled across her mind. *How perfect that would be. But where would I find such a gown?* Just then there was a loud thud that caused Janet to sit up on her bed. She looked around to see if a picture or something had fallen, but all looked fine. *Hmm, that's strange. I guess I might as well get up and find some way to redeem the hole I've made for myself.* She put her feet on the floor to stand up. *Ohhh, what's this?*

Janet looked down and on the floor was the journal. How did that get there? She could have sworn that she had placed it back in the trunk. She picked it up and the cover of the journal warmed in her hands. *Strange. So strange.*

"Use my wedding dress."

The voice she heard was how she had imagined Clarissa's voice to sound as she had read the journal entries. *No, that's not possible. It's the stress of the moment.*

Janet put the thought out of her head and proceeded to the bathroom to wash and get ready for a day of excursions to find something to wear to the ball. She walked in and looked at her image in the mirror. For a fleeting second, she saw herself in a claret ball gown, hair tied up with claret ribbon and a claret masquerade mask complete with a feather. Janet blinked and it was gone. *Get a grip, Janet. This isn't worth losing your mind over.*

"Use my wedding dress." Clarissa's voice seemed to be audible and reverberating around the tiled walls of the bathroom.

Janet shook her head, not believing what she just audibly heard. She turned and went back into the bedroom. The trunk lid was raised, and the muslin pulled back, revealing the wedding gown. Suddenly, it was like a light turned on in Janet's mind. *Yes! I can dye the dress claret to match the ribbon around the poem, take my white gloves and dye them to match. I can get shoes that can be dyed, and I'll have my vintage ball gown. No one will suspect that it was a wedding dress. It will be perfect, and I can get it all done in just a week.*

Janet spun around and around her bedroom like she was waltzing with a tall, dark, and handsome stranger who would sweep her off her feet like Charles had done with Clarissa. She fell giggling onto the bed, speaking out her joy. "As fate would have it, thanks Mom and Dad for buying that trunk so many years ago. You just saved my job, and the museum will get a hefty donation from Mr. Richard Alexander Petrovich."

Jumping off the bed, Janet grabbed some comfy clothing for trekking off to the museum and the making of a matching dye using the poem's ribbon for the color match. Life was looking up.

After getting dressed, Janet scarfed a coffee and a quick pastry. She put on her gloves and found the scroll buried in the pouch. She untied the scroll and immediately it opened as if it had never been rolled up. She was always astounded at how that could be. Janet's eyes skimmed the poem again. It had been a while since she had first read it.

> *If You Dare*
> *Wear it if you dare — Wear it and become fair.*
> *Wear it if you suffer — Wear it as your buffer.*
> *Through new eyes you will see — just who God created you to be.*
> *Watch what a new view will do — Transformation into the new you.*
> *Trust the Mask and lose the past.*
> *Life will take on purpose and meaning — The truths of life will reveal*
> *   your inner being.*
> *Time and circumstances brought the Mask to your hand —*
> *Wear it and find your special Godly man.*
> *His love will forever be only for you — Trust the Mask and say, "I*
> *   do."*
> *Love awaits, make no mistake*
> *The passing of time has brought your season —*
> *To move forward, you must give up logic and reason.*

Janet's reading of the poem brought some very strange thoughts. *Could there be a force behind the story of Clarissa and Charles?*

Were the fables or legends told by Abigail true? She didn't know what to think. She was a logical gal and nothing about the stories in the journal were logical. They were almost to be considered miraculous. But when Janet read the poem a second time, some words jumped out at her like they were neon and flashing.

Time and circumstances brought the Mask to your hand...

The passing of time has brought your season – To move forward, you must give up logic and reason.

The words tumbled over and over in her mind. *Time and circumstances have brought the Mask to your hand.* Janet put these words with the journal stories. Abigail had been captured before the Mask could change her life by marrying the love of her life. She didn't have a chance to have her destiny fulfilled. She saw what could have been when Efosa declared he would marry her. Circumstances altered Abigail's options forever, including those of her family line. The Mask had come half a world over to be given to Clarissa through circumstances only a supreme being who controlled fates and destiny could achieve. The statistical likelihood of all these things lining up were just too high. Abigail and her sons escaped and found their way to the one branch of the Underground Railroad that had a stop at Clarissa's house. Clarissa and her father taking Abigail in and developing a relationship allowed Abigail to trust her inheritance of the Mask to someone outside of her tribe and lineage. All the coincidences that just happened to align that led to Clarissa and Charles meeting on that New Year's Eve ball and knowing they were fated to be the love of each other and soulmates through life. The fact that they never had children and that the Mask remained hidden in the trunk with the journal and scroll until Russell bought the trunk for Louise. Yet they had left it and now Janet was in possession of the trunk, journal, the Mask, and dress. The odds just kept getting more staggering. Janet in her logic knew human intervention could not have orchestrated this. Only a supreme being who had allowed the creation of such a destiny-changing Mask could be behind it.

"Do you hear what you are thinking?" Janet spoke out loud to herself. "If these things are beyond the normal ability to just happen, then that means this supernatural being has also determined for me to be touched by His favor. That is humbling to think about." She paused and felt the halls of eternity were full of people who were aware of her in this moment and rooting for her to move forward, giving up logic and reason…and trusting!

"God, I guess I have never really given You much thought. But I do believe that You exist and that somehow and some way, You deemed me the one to experience the life change of the Mask."

Janet took a deep sigh and felt all the stress leave her. Instead, she began to feel excitement for the unknown destiny, and apparently the unknown man who was going to come into her life at some point. As surely as the Mask and dress had all come into her hands, God was pulling her now towards a destiny that was going to be more than she could ever imagine. In that moment, Janet knew that she would wear the Mask to the New Year's Eve Ball, and she prayed that the man God had for her would soon appear in her life.

Having made that decision, Janet gathered her purse, the claret ribbon, and the gloves. December was chilly but sunny today and the walk to the underground train station would be a brisk one but enjoyable with just a lightweight coat. The museum was only a few stops down the line. Janet smiled at the thought that she was about to ride on a literal underground railroad. Life has a way of repeating itself.

"That is just too much!" Janet laughed as she locked her door and started out for the museum. Today she would create the solution for a vintage dress. Then she would take the risk and wear the Mask and the dress for the New Year's Eve Ball.

Chapter 8
History Repeats Itself

New Year's Eve
London Apartment

Janet had managed once again to cinch up the corset, add the underlying petticoats, and pull on the stockings. *I understand the need for personal assistants when women wore these things. I could work up a sweat just trying to layer it all.* Her hair had responded to the curling iron, but not as much as she'd hoped. The claret ribbon from the scroll worked perfect to pull up one side of her hair. She styled it just like Clarissa's description in the journal. The ribbon had helped her create the perfect color and shade of dye for the dress, gloves, and shoes. She soaked the wedding dress and gloves the following week, but let the shoe store dye the shoes with a bottle of dye she provided. The dress had air dried on a form, and then she had painstakingly steamed each layer of lace and satin. The dress was a magnificent red that resembled the warm deep color of the wine produced in the Bordeaux region of France. It might be a new color for the dress, but the hue complimented the dress and the combination spoke of a time long ago when details were everything.

Janet took the dress off the hanger and stepped into it so she wouldn't muss her hair and makeup. It took a while for all the underlying layers to behave and layer themselves as they were designed to do. The buttons on the bodice were another issue. Thankfully, she had brought home a button hook from the museum, a gadget to help button long rows of buttons. Without it, she knew her fingers would have been cramping. All was complete. Now it was time for her to see just what kind of powers the Mask held. She knew from Clarissa's vivid journal entries that once she put the Mask on, if she was the intended receiver, it would somehow disappear and no one would ever see it, feel it or know it was on her face. Clarissa had detailed that when Charles took her face in his hands and began to caress it and kiss it from her forehead toward her bosom, he never knew that she was wearing the Mask. It was her secret and she never removed it until after Charles had died.

Now was the moment of truth. Would the Mask accept her as its next fated owner, or would it reject her? If it did reject her, she would have a very weighty decision to make about where the Mask would end up. "Lord, I believe that You have passed this to me. I pray that all the words of the poem will come true."

She picked up the Mask, put it to her face, and pulled it snug. Then weaving the strings through her hair and tying them fast, she let her hair tumble over them. Before she could fluff her hair, she felt a warm, curious sensation. At first it was just the tip of her nose and chin, but it continued and spread. She whirled around, headed toward the bathroom, and gazed at herself in the mirror. The Mask was working, disappearing into her skin. The Mask had accepted her as its next receiver of special powers. The process was totally amazing and somewhat shocking to think that it would be on her face going forward until the conditions Clarissa talked about were met. Finally, the warm and tingling sensations abated. Janet stepped closer to the mirror as much as her dress with layers of petticoats and crinolines allowed. Her face had indeed taken on a radiance and a glow, just as Clarissa had described. Her features somehow transformed, she looked at her new appearance and laughed.

"Girl, you look fabulous even if I do say so myself." She laughed as she spoke to herself.

Janet continued her appraisal. Yep, her bosom was fuller and even higher. Her waist was narrower, and it felt like the corset was even looser. She couldn't tell about her hips because the dress covered everything from the narrow waist down to her matching claret shoes. Her normal subdued personality felt perky and adventurous. Yes, the legend was true. She was living proof and there wasn't a soul she would dare to share it with. Who would believe it, anyway? There were evil people in this world who would want to steal it for themselves or cut it up and test it for a new beauty cream and make millions. No, the secret must be hers until it was passed on to her daughter or the next person God would direct, if a daughter was not in her future. Finally, she looked at her hair and, just like Clarissa's, it had more volume and bounce to it. She laughed to herself and thought she should have saved her efforts with the curling iron. Under the bathroom lights, it even looked like it had some sun-drenched highlights.

"Well God, let me wear the Mask and live out my life as You have planned for me. Help me be like Clarissa and be one to make a difference in so many lives. Let me have the wisdom to know when I find my Mr. Right."

As Janet put on lipstick that matched the color of her dress, she also realized that her lips were a little poutier, a validation of another journal entry. Janet grabbed her gloves and put them on, then wrapped the fur cloak she had found in an antique clothing boutique around her shoulders. Lastly, she picked up the masquerade mask, which was secured to a stick. It too had been created from claret-colored sequins glued to the plastic mask. It covered her eyes, nose, and flared up toward her temples. A plume of claret-colored feathers completed it. She walked slowly and felt a difference in her gait that the Mask had created. It was like she floated across the floor. Locking her door, Janet placed her door key, a credit card, her ID and her lipstick in a deep hidden pocket she had found in the folds of the skirt when she was steaming it. The museum had hired a limo service to take all the employees to the ball, so none of them had to fuss with money, subway travel, or indulging in too much alcohol. The limo was waiting at the curb.

The chauffeur did a double take as Janet glided toward the vehicle. "May I say, ma'am, you look stunning tonight? Certainly, you will be the belle of the ball."

"Thank you, kind sir." Janet laughed as she pushed her crinolines and petticoats into the entire backseat. The exertion wasn't lost on the driver, who smiled as he peered at her in the rearview mirror.

9 PM
New Year's Eve Ball
1st Floor Lobby
Grosvenor House, London

Janet instructed the limo driver to take her to a side door of the hotel to avoid all the red-carpet media frenzy. Although she felt emboldened by the Mask, she still wanted to avoid the crush of the media's celebrity coverage. The marketing team had surpassed all expectations and the fundraiser seemed to be the event to be seen attending. Janet preferred the obscurity or normalcy, so she had scouted out the secondary entrance when she had toured the facility. Yesterday she had confirmed that the side entrance would be accessible as she did her final inspection. Checking the room layout, seating cards and the pièces de resistance, the wedding gown and dress uniform that Queen Victoria and Prince Albert wore on their wedding day, Janet knew the ball should go off without any problems.

She had the ballroom designed in a large 360-degree layout. The dinner tables were placed in staggered arrangements around the outside ballroom walls. This made three large circles with each table having an unhindered view of the dance floor and the center display. The tables were more intimate by hugging the walls, as well as separation from the dance area created by the central open space. The crown jewel, the display of the Royal wedding attire, was placed on a large dais in the very center. The accent lighting illuminated the beautiful Royal garments, so every detail was visible. It was magnificent. The display slowly turned so that anyone in the ballroom would be able to see the spectacular exhibit, the foundation piece for the new wing. The fundraiser would provide the permanent display not only for these national treasures, but for all the historic pieces that had been donated and collected so far. Hopefully, tonight's fundraiser would provide the funds for the building as well as excess funding for procurement of new treasures.

Although Janet tried to be inconspicuous as she moved to the elevator, hitting the up button to the second-floor ballroom, amazed eyes noticed the red vintage ball gown and the beautiful woman wearing it. Women stared and men smiled.

"Look, Mommy, there is a lady like in my storybook. She must be a princess. I want to go see her." The little girl excitedly let go of her mother's hand and ran across the lobby area, crashing into Janet with a big, attempted hug around her legs that would have knocked her down if two strong arms had not grabbed her in that moment. The elevator door had opened just as a gentleman stepped out—an off-balance Janet fell back into his arms as her heel landed on his foot.

Embarrassed by the attention and what must have been painful for the gentleman, Janet squeaked out, "Oh, I'm so sorry. I hope your foot is okay." Without turning her head to make facial contact, Janet found her balance as the little girl continued to squeeze into the petticoats and crinolines with joyful giggles at meeting a "real" princess

"The foot's okay, and I'm glad I could be of help." The voice caused goosebumps to pop up on Janet's skin. His words had been said with a hint of humor in his voice that reached down inside of her and bounced around, bombarding her heart.

"Mommy! Come and see the princess. Isn't she beautiful, and look…she has a prince with her!"

The mother arrived and apologized for her daughter's behavior as she tried to pry her loose from Janet's legs and dress. "Now Nancy, tell the nice lady you are sorry for almost making her fall."

"I'm sorry, princess. I just wanted to meet you and tell my friends that I really did meet a real princess."

Now that there was no more danger of falling, Janet laughed without thinking and said, "Would you like a picture with me?"

The little girl turned to her mother, "Please, Mommy, please? And can we take it with your prince too?"

"Well, her prince would love to be in the picture with both of you." The goosebump-inducing voice gave a deep, jovial laugh that caused Janet's legs to go wobbly…thankfully she caught herself before falling.

She turned slowly to look at this "prince" to see who he was and why she was reacting to his voice like this. The first thing she saw was that he was taller than her 5´5" because her eye level came to the middle of his broad chest. He was wearing a vintage military cape that parted in the middle, revealing an army officer uniform complete with medals. Janet's gaze quickly went upward and met the gentle smile of a man with dark, thick, wavy hair, a matching dark, thick moustache, long sideburns, and dark brown eyes to drown in. Suddenly she remembered her dream. This was the literal man of her dreams. She blinked and swallowed at the surprise. He caught the slow flush on her cheeks and his smile widened.

"Sir Richard Alexander Petrovich at your service, my princess." He took her gloved hand, raised it to his lips, and kissed her knuckles. She felt the warmth of his breath through her gloves. Janet heard the little girl giggle.

"Mommy, it's just like my book. The prince kisses the princess's hand, and they get married and live happily ever after! Are you getting married tonight?"

Janet was speechless. It was like all the air had left her lungs. She was lightheaded and afraid she would swoon.

"Does the princess have a name?" he asked.

Janet gulped and breathed in some much-needed air. Slowly she got her words out. "The princess's name is Janet."

"Does the princess have a last name?" As he said this, he took her by the arm and turned to face the mother and daughter, who were waiting for a picture. "My I pick up your daughter for the picture?"

"Please, Mommy, please!"

"All right, as long as you promise to smile and not make any more demands on these good people's time."

"Yes, Mommy. I will behave."

Janet's prince scooped the little girl up into his arms and then stepped sideways, placing an arm around Janet's waist, pulling her close to his side. The air left her lungs again as she contacted with his left side. His arm tightened and steadied her.

Alexander looked down at her and winked. Then he smiled at the phone and the other people who had stopped for this photo op as well. He looked back at Janet and said, "Smile your beautiful smile so that they get a good picture of what our family will look like one day."

Before Janet could turn her head and ask what he was talking about, the cameras started flashing and phones went off. It seemed that avoiding the media hadn't worked. By now the London Press and other reporters had a picture of her and Sir Richard Alexander Petrovich and their staged family. Janet closed her eyes and prayed her face in the photos didn't look like a deer in the headlights or her mouth gaping open in shock at his words.

9:20 PM
2nd Floor Ballroom

Janet had managed to slip away after the embarrassing unexpected photo op, as Sir Alexander was bombarded with press for statements about his new business ventures in container shipping and his latest sale of real estate along the Danube to a winery. She quickly made her way to the ballroom, checked her fur cloak, and found Vickey and the others to see how all was going. Forty-five minutes remained before the start of dinner, and it appeared that three-fourths of the guests had already arrived, checked in, and were enjoying the cocktails and appetizers. People were decked out in their vintage outfits, mingling, and socializing around the room.

With everything under control and Vickey telling her to go and just enjoy the night, Janet strolled slowly around the room, talking to people she had met before and smiling at those she hadn't, praying that everyone opened their pockets and lavished the museum with the funds to complete the project. Sometimes, she felt like there was a warm caress on her exposed neck but chalked it up to her nerves. A lot was riding on the success of this event. Being away from Mr. Richard Alexander Pertrovich, Janet's pulse had returned to normal, and she could breathe. She pushed the events in the lobby out of her mind. If she didn't, her body would start to react as if he was standing beside her. As she continued to stroll around the ballroom, Janet suddenly found herself in front of a full-length mirror. Suddenly, it was like déjà vu. She froze as she gazed at her reflection in the mirror. This was the very picture she had seen back in Ohio in her room. The Mask was and had been at work.

At precisely 10 o'clock, the soft orchestra music stopped, and Vickey appeared in the center of the ballroom. She asked everyone to find their designated seats because dinner was about to be served. A cheer went up and people quickly found their seats. Janet had avoided her table because she knew that Sir Alexander had been placed there. She slowly maneuvered through the three rows of tables to her table placed snuggly back in a corner near the wall. Much to her unsettled feelings, Sir Alexander stood with her chair pulled out, waiting to seat her.

"I took the liberty of moving my seating card beside yours, since we have already been introduced as the princess and her prince."

Janet blushed again and looked down away from his intense brown eyes and took her seat. She took a moment to adjust the crinolines and petticoats down and under the table. Sir Alexander sat down and offered to fill her water goblet. She nodded because her words were stuck in her throat. She finally got out, "Thank you," and promptly turned her attention to the couple to her left, frequent visitors to the museum and faithful donors any time the museum had a need. They would keep her busy in conversation.

Janet managed to finish her dinner without having any conversation with Sir Alexander. He seemed to be using his time to talk business with two of the men on his right. What was it about this man that turned her inside out? *Where is the confidence and the buffer that the Mask is supposed to bring me, according to the poem? Right now, all I feel is that my once secure world has been tilted on its axis and things are going to spin out of control.*

The orchestra began to tune up and Vickey came back to the center to speak. "What a wonderful meal. Special thanks goes out to Janet Rush for the menu selection. Now we can start the dancing!" The crowd erupted into spontaneous light applause. "The tables will be cleared, and the desserts, hot and cold drinks and liqueurs will be available where the appetizers had been located. Feel free to get your desserts when you are ready. We have placed donation envelops at your table. Please give generously for this great new wing for our Victoria and Albert Museum. We are most grateful to the Royal family who donated the marriage outfits of Queen Victoria and Prince Albert to the museum in good faith that your contributions tonight will build a first-class display, allowing the museum to not only display them, but an entire bridal wing collection. You can place your donation envelope with your generous contribution in this beautiful crystal box which we will leave right here in the center of the dance floor. Now who will be the first to drop in their donation?"

Janet looked around — it seemed that everyone was pulling out their checks from pockets and purses and placing them in the donation envelopes. The orchestra struck up with the Viennese Waltz. Couples stood up and began making their way to the donation box and then took off waltzing. Janet kept her back to Sir Alexander. She was afraid that if she had to dance with him, she'd be unable to stand, let alone waltz. Just the thought of his warm hands on her waist and his strong arms pulling her close made her legs feel like jelly. Her head was already dizzy from his cologne. *What is wrong with me? Why am I feeling like this? It must be the Mask. I'm not as strong as Clarissa and its powers are affecting me. Maybe I should go get some air.*

Janet went to push her chair back to stand up with all her layers of petticoats and crinolines, but her actions were already anticipated. Sir Alexander was up and pulling out her chair.

"Are you ready for your first waltz of the night, Ms. Rush — or should I call you 'princess'? My 'princess'?"

Janet's head pivoted sharply towards him as his words, 'My princess,' reached her slow-working, foggy brain.

Sir Alex laughed. "I see you're perplexed by my words."

Janet felt swallowed up, looking into his dark eyes. She was slowly sinking into warm quicksand and didn't care. Her heart was beating fast, and she was breathless. He put his index finger softly upon her lips as if to silence any response. His eyes were looking at her lips and she wanted him to kiss her in the most desperately wicked way.

"Let's take a walk." He didn't give Janet time to answer. He took a gentle hold on her arm at the elbow, and they walked out into the second-floor lobby, heading to a quiet nook nestled behind the elevators. He didn't say a word as they walked but being with him was enough for Janet. She felt hopelessly captivated and joyously infatuated with this man. As they approached the seating area, the sequined masquerade mask Janet had clutched so tightly from the moment he had pulled out her chair fell from her now very relaxed hand. As she watched it fall in slow motion, in her head, she heard Clarissa's voice clearly. It was as if Clarissa was standing beside her, speaking into her ear. *"It's the Mask. All that you are feeling is the result of your awakened passion and desire for this man you are destined to marry. Remember the poem. It is never wrong. Time and circumstance brought the Mask to your hand. Wear it and find your special godly man. His love will forever be only for you. Trust the Mask and say, 'I do.' Love awaits, make no mistake."*

Janet giggled as she sat down. She had no doubts now. All things were in action because of the Mask. Her nerves calmed and she turned to look Sir Alexander square in his eyes. He immediately saw the change in her demeanor and smiled, relaxing his shoulders. He still held her arm as if he was afraid she would bolt like a skittish colt.

"Sir Alexander, I think…"

"Call me Alex."

"All right, Alex, I think it's time you finally kissed me."

Pleased, Alex let out a hearty laugh and without hesitation, pulled her tight into his arms. Then he started kissing her forehead, cheeks, nose, slowing working down to her lips. He softly moved his lips across hers, then kissed her passionately. It was a kiss that would rival any romance scene from a hot steamy novel.

"I have been waiting weeks to do that."

"Weeks? What do you mean? We met just a few hours ago."

"True, but I first saw you in my dreams back in the spring. You are the woman in my dreams. I know it sounds so much like a cliché, but you were and are. In my first dream you were far away, but I could see you with your hair full of cobwebs and bug shells. You had dirt streaked across your face. Sunlight was streaming in around you and you were the most adorable woman I had ever seen. In fact, your dirty face and cobwebbed hair showed me that you were not like most women I know. They wouldn't touch anything that might make them dirty or break a manicured fingernail. When I awoke, all I could do was wonder who you were and if you really existed. I feared you were just an apparition of my mind that had stirred a yearning for a love that was more than I had ever known. If you were, I would have wanted to live my life in that dream." He laughed at how silly it sounded, yet how desperate he had been.

Janet froze—not because of his obsession with her dream image, but from the vision of her own experiences in the spring. She had been in her parents' attic and had found the trunk. His dream vision would have matched what she probably looked like in the attic, cobwebs, and all. That was the night she found the journal and dreamed of an elusive man who had been searching for her. It had to be the workings of the Mask. Somehow, some way, the Mask had shown Alex her dirt-smudged face in a dream and had stirred his passion for only her. It didn't make sense, but she knew that what they were feeling was the beginning of a lifelong passion, promised by the Mask. She had dreamed of him for the first time that night too.

"Earth to Janet."

His voice brought her back to the present. The Mask was her secret. But she knew what was at work. She smiled, held his face in her hands and pulled him close for another passionate kiss.

"You feel it too, don't you?" Alex's question was sincere, and he looked relieved, yet amazed. His voice trembled as he spoke of what was happening between them.

Had he worried that when he met her, she would not reciprocate his passionate connection? Janet didn't want him to worry. She was just as passionate. Laughing, Janet said, "I saw you, or glimpses of you, in dreams as well. But God apparently gave you more info on me than He did me for you."

Alex continued with a strong and sincere voice. "This connection is more than physical attraction. It's a tie that goes beyond the normal. I can't explain it and I can't make sense of it. Trust me—I have tried. Logical explanations can't account for it. It is spiritual and supernatural. Now don't laugh, but I prayed to God after the dreams started and told Him that I would love this woman of my dreams until I died if He brought her across my path. I started going to the little church in my village and when I prayed, I felt God's love and I felt more and more love for you. I talked to the minister because I thought I might be losing my mind. The dreams were nightly, and each night I couldn't wait to fall asleep to see you and experience your smile and your laughter."

"What did the minister say about it all?"

"He said that God can have a perfect soul mate and partner for us and that together we complete and bring out the best in each other. He said that God ordains destinies and paths to cross for His purposes. I knew then you were that woman. Only you could I love with all my being. The only love that I wanted was attached to your face. I began to travel and search the crowds, the papers, the magazines for just a glimpse of the woman I was dreaming about. Where would I find her? Now don't laugh, but as the dreams continued, I saw our life unfold with a love that was so strong and passionate, that I would ache for you to be in my arms. You know that little girl we took the picture with?"

Janet could only nod.

"Well, I saw us with a son and a daughter. Two beautiful children in a beautiful and fulfilled life."

As Janet sat and listened to his words, tears streamed down her face. This was the stuff of novels or Hollywood films. Yet a woman over a hundred years ago — no, women over the millenniums — had experienced a love that only God could create and kindle. Love that Solomon wrote about in the Song of Solomon as recorded in the Bible. Destinies had crossed paths, and all because of the Mask. A wedding gift thousands of years ago had set things in motion. Now she was going to be a part of that legacy. How did she get to be so lucky to find the Mask? No! The Mask had found her.

"Tell me more Alex, how did you find me?"

"A friend of mine told me about this fundraiser and knew that this would be something I would want to donate to. He hoped it would be a distraction to snap me out of my crazy behavior. He had seen how I would mope around at times and my interest in the fairer sex was totally gone. I stopped socializing. He was worried about me and showed me the London paper that had a spread on the fundraiser. There on the page with the proposed new wing for the Victoria and Albert Museum was your picture as the new curator of exhibits for the bridal wing. I couldn't believe it. I had finally found you. I have been planning this night out for months, ever since the day I saw you in the newspaper picture. Do you know how hard it was to not just show up at your door before tonight?"

"Oh, I'm so glad you didn't." Janet's mind processed the possible results. *I wouldn't have put on the Mask at that point and so I might not have reacted as I did tonight. I could have told him to get lost.* Janet just smiled, keeping her thoughts to herself. *Thank You, God!*

"Janet Rush, will you be my wife?"

Without hesitation, Janet answered, "Yes! Sir Richard Alexander Petrovich. A thousand times, yes!"

"When? Now that I have kissed you and held you in my arms, I am not sure I can wait and keep my hands off you."

Janet blushed. Grabbing his face, she kissed him with equal passion.

Someone walked by from the restrooms and cleared his throat, interrupting them before an inevitable tumble to the floor.

"We should go back into the ballroom and distract ourselves from these erupting passions," Alex choked out.

Janet giggled as they stood up, recovering themselves, and reached out her hand. "Sir Alexander Petrovich, I do believe you owe me a waltz."

He grabbed her hand and pulled her close for one more kiss before stepping onto the ballroom dance floor. From shoulders to toes, their body heat mingled and ignited.

"Miss Rush, I'm going to need a cold shower if we don't get out on the dance floor."

They purposefully danced every dance: hip hop, disco, tango, waltz, you name it. Whatever song the orchestra played, they danced it or laughed through it as they tried to follow the steps. People took notice that they only had eyes and sometimes hands for each other.

11:55 PM
2nd Floor Ballroom

Vickey signaled for a drum roll after the last dance, and

everyone turned to give her their attention.

"Ladies and gentlemen, on behalf of the Victoria and Albert Museum, we want to thank you for attending tonight and making this event such a success. We are pleased to tell you that we not only met but nearly doubled the contributions for our fundraising needs. We can start construction on the new wing in the spring. With your generous donations, we will be able to purchase many unique wedding collections from around the world. It will be a one-of-a-kind museum for sure. Now it is time I see for our countdown into the new year. So, get your glasses filled with the champagne that is on the tables and let's count down to the New Year!"

"Eight, Seven, Six, Five, Four, Three, Two, One, Happy New Year!" The ballroom guests all shouted together, then clinked their glasses with those around them and sipped the bubbly champagne.

"Miss Rush, I do believe that's our signal to leave, and your chariot awaits to take you home."

"Why, thank you, kind sir. I have danced my feet off and I'm ready to take off my shoes and this dress."

Alex's eyes got big, and he quickly said, "That's not what I was getting at. I've waited all this time, I will wait a little longer even though I can say several cold showers will be my daily routine until we are married."

Janet laughed. "I understand believe me. My comments were not meant as a tease or a hint to see what your reactions were. I am an old-fashioned girl, and as much as you make me want to melt into your luscious body, I too will restrain myself."

They both laughed and moved to get their coats. Alex had a private limo, which came to the side door and picked them up. Alex told the driver Janet's address—she looked at him and they both started laughing.

"You weren't kidding when you said you had wanted to show up at my door. You know where I live."

"Yes, once I found out who you were I found out everything about you. I know your parents are Russell and Louise Rush. I know all things, Janet. I even know about a crush on someone named Liam."

"And you still want to marry me?" Janet asked, laughing. Yet even as she laughed, she wondered. If he knew so much about the details of her life, how boring and mundane her life had been, how amazing that he, a man with such social presence and money would still want to marry her.

"Nothing except your refusal will stop me. You are beautiful, confident, responsible, ethical, caring about others, and would sacrifice whatever it took for those you love. You are exactly what I need and want."

"Well, sir, if you have seen and know all that I am, and still want me, then this lady will become your princess for as long as you want her."

"There's no fear of me ever changing my mind. I want you more than life itself. You make me complete!"

Alex pulled her close in the back seat and they made out like two teenagers. Alex had to make his hands behave and he just sighed and pulled her even closer to calm the rising tide of passion he was feeling. Janet was thankful for his control because she was at the brink of losing hers.

Too soon they arrived at Janet's apartment and the limo driver waited until he saw that their embrace was beginning to disentangle.

"Sir, are you going in? Should I wait?"

"No." "Yes." Janet and Alex answered at the same time. They laughed and so did the driver.

"You want me to come in? I'm not sure that is wise." Alex said sincerely.

"Alex, as much as I desire in the strongest way to have you spend the night, I think we need to talk about all of this. It is a little fast even though I believe with all my heart that we are meant to be together. I think we should talk family, future and wedding. There is so much I don't know about you, and I want to know everything. I want to walk down the aisle knowing your deepest secrets, your passions, and your dreams. How about we spend the night talking into the New Year about our new life?"

Alex smiled. "I just love you more and more. John, you can let us out and come back in the morning about 9:00 AM and you can drive us to breakfast. Please tell Larry what I'm doing and that he can send with you some clothes and my grooming bag."

"Yes sir."

Alex got out and helped Janet out with her full dress. They

walked up the stairs to her apartment and went in.

"Feel free to take off your formal jacket and shoes. Get comfy, because I'm going to ask you a thousand questions. I'm going to get out of this gown and change into some sweats and my slippers. Then prepare, Mr. Petrovich, for the interrogation is about to begin."

"You can investigate all aspects of my life. My life is open before you. I don't want any secrets between us." Alex was so sincere; it almost made her cry.

"I love you, Alex." It was said with such simplicity and truth. Janet sweetly kissed him and started to turn to go change.

Alex grabbed her hand and pulled her close. "And I love you Janet Rush, forever." It was said with the same simple truth. He kissed her back just as tenderly.

9:00AM
New Year's Day
London Apartment

Alex's phone startled them both awake. For a second they each didn't know where they were, but seeing that they had fallen asleep, snuggled into a curled-up, nesting position on the couch brought laughter. Alex reached for his phone and answered it.

"Hello, John. Can you park the car and bring up my things?"

Janet stood up and stretched and started to walk to the bathroom, but Alex caught her hand and pulled her down onto his lap.

"Good morning, soon-to-be Mrs. Richard Alexander Petrovich. I slept so good with you next to me. No dreams. Just blissful sleep."

He took her face into his hands and kissed her, pushing her tousled hair out of her face.

"I will never grow tired of waking up with you next to me." Alex smiled as he spoke.

"You say the nicest things, but I gotta go! Really Alex, I've gotta go!" She kissed him back quickly with a peck on his lips and ran to the bathroom.

Alex laughed and answered the chauffeur's knock at the door. John carried in Alex's change of clothes and grooming bag, and took a seat.

10:00 AM
London Apartment

"I have to say, Miss Rush, that I love you even more when it comes to getting ready—you are a woman with a purpose, and there is no dallying with decisions. I love it. Everything I find out about you makes me love you more. How does The Wolseley sound for brunch?"

"Why Mr. Petrovich, I can say that you are a man who cleans up pretty good yourself and The Wolseley is perfect. I have heard the food is five star. But will they be open?"

"First off. Pretty good? I was hoping for a little more on my brute appeal. And I told you I had planned for this time. Yes, they are open for special clients."

"Well sir, I don't want you to think too highly of yourself."

"Sorry, Miss Rush, but since I have the girl of my dreams on my arm and she has said yes to marry me, I'm already on cloud nine."

"If I'm honest, I'd have to say you are the most handsome man alive. And the fact that you love me and went to all the effort to meet, sweep me off my feet, and plan this day, makes me the luckiest woman in the world."

They laughed and kissed while John just smiled and locked the door as they all went out.

"Here are your keys, miss."

Janet laughed and put them in her purse. "Thanks, John, for looking out for me."

"No problem, ma'am. I figure that will become one of my new jobs soon."

Alex and Janet laughed. John smiled and opened the door to the back seat.

The drive to the restaurant took about thirty minutes in traffic. Janet was thankful for the holiday and the day off to spend with Alex. He held her close in his arms and she rested her head on his shoulder. They were talked out. The had covered just about everything in their all-night conversations until falling asleep somewhere about 4:30 in the morning.

Janet looked up at Alex and pulled back to see his full face.

"Alex, when do you want to get married? My parents can come anytime. But when do you want to get married?

"Babe, you know that today would be just fine with me, but the wedding is a big deal for the bride, and I want you to plan our wedding, so that it is what you want."

"Well, you know that Queen Victoria and Prince Albert got married on February 10th and they are part of the reason that we found each other. I read a historical journal about a couple that were brought together in almost an identical story as ours. They also met on New Year's Eve at a ball. It was love at first sight you could say for them too. They got married on Valentine's Day. So, what do you think about February 12th, that's right in the middle to get married?"

"Like I said, we could go today before a judge or the mayor and I'd be just fine, but you plan this for your dreams."

Janet closed her eyes and thought about Clarissa and Charles. She thought about Abigail and all the others who were connected to her happiness. A tear came to her eye.

Alex was quick to see it. "Hey, what's wrong? Did I say something I shouldn't have said?"

"No, I am just so happy. February 12th will be perfect. It will give Mom time to get her dress. It will give us time to get a venue, plan the details and who will be invited. I know it is forty-three days out, but you have made it this long, can you wait another forty-three days? I have some great ideas for a Victorian-themed wedding. It just seems fitting with all that has happened."

"Having your love in my life for as long as I live, which by the way I plan to live to a ripe old age, I think I can wait a few more weeks. For now, I will satisfy my hunger with The Wolseley's Eggs Benedict and some waffles. But my lips are in need of yours right now, so Miss Rush, kiss me."

As Janet leaned into Alex and they kissed a slow passionate kiss, she knew she was going to start her journal today so that all the details for her daughter would not be forgotten. She wanted her journal to record all the details in her journey with the love of her life. One day, she would add her journal to Clarissa's and hand them over along with the Mask to her daughter. Then her daughter could carry on the legacy of the Mask for another generation.

As the kiss ended, Alex kissed her forehead, and Janet leaned back into his arms.

"John?"

"Yes ma'am?"

"Is there a stationary store near where we are going to eat?"

"Yes ma'am."

"Good. When we leave, I would like to go there if it is open and get a journal and some other things to start planning our wedding."

"Journal?" Alex questioned her. "What do you need one of those for?"

"Well, you must admit, our relationship was divinely inspired. In just twenty-four hours so many things have taken place in our relationship. I don't want to forget one detail. One day, our daughter will marry, and she should understand just what kind of supernatural power can exist and operate when God and the passing of heritage come together."

Alex pulled her close and whispered in her ear. "Just leave out the hot part. We don't want to get her hopes up that she will find what we have. What we have is so very rare."

"Oh, I don't think she will have any problem finding her forever perfect love either. I'm sure that what we have been blessed with will come to her, too. She will find her special godly man and his love for her will be a forever love, just like her father has for her mother and she for him."

Alex's eyes twinkled down at Janet as he smiled.

"She can trust the Ma…" Janet pulled the rest of the word back in quickly and kept talking. She had almost revealed a secret that was hers alone until she passed it on. "She can trust the man that God will bring to her, and she will be able to say 'I do' with the full confidence that her marriage will be a lifetime adventure just like ours. 'Love awaits, make no mistake'."

Alex held Janet's face in his hands. Looking intently into her eyes, he whispered, "You, Janet Toupes, complete me. From the moment I saw you in my dreams, I was hopelessly in love with you. There will never be another woman who will have my total and undivided love. It is forever."

Janet closed her eyes and savored the feel of his hands, knowing that the Mask was at work and would be forever in the blessed lives of those it chose. Destinies awaited.

END

***House of the Four Pillars**

The House of the Four Pillars is on the National Register of Historic Places. Based on oral histories, this home was part of the Underground Railroad. The Toledo area was a critical layover for slaves escaping to freedom before the Civil War. The region was a direct link from Kentucky and Indiana to Michigan and Canada. It is marker #5 on the Ohio Literary Trail.

Betty is a member of AFCW, WW, CIPA, AWSA. Publications include The River; A Spiritually Transforming Journey, *and winner of the CIPA Awards for General Fiction, two Guidepost devotionals, and a devotional in the anthology* Radical Abundance: More Than All We Can Ask or Imagine.

BOOKS: CAGED AND FREE
By Michelle L. Levigne

Tonight, the last librarian stayed later than usual. The patrons had left just before 9pm, in a hurry to escape the approaching rainstorm, or urged out by quietly voiced announcements of the time, and requests to please take their books to the checkout desk. In the chatter of saying goodbye, shutting down computer terminals, checking that chairs were pushed up under the reading tables and turning off lights in different portions of the building, none of the other staff had noticed the quietly building hum in the air. The sense of growing alertness. That hush of anticipation similar to when seconds turned into minutes and even hours in a crucial play in a ball game.

The last librarian noticed. Several times she raised her head from the proofs she was checking, preparing materials for the end of the summer reading program and the preparation for back-to-school activities. Each time, she glanced toward the lobby, positive that someone was there, trying to get in through the locked doors, waving for attention, but not knocking.

Each time she looked up, however, she didn't look long enough to notice that the light slanting through the windows at the front of the building, and the windows in the doors, wasn't at the right angle to come from the parking lot lights. The growing rumble of the strengthening downpour on the roof distracted her. She thought more about how she was going to get from the security door to her car fifty feet away without getting drenched. She had an umbrella, but had left it in her car. She didn't notice the light had a faint greenish-bluish tint, rather than the rain-washed yellow of the parking lot lights. Other nights when she stayed a little later after everyone else had left and the library was locked up, she had partially noticed, but shrugged it off as moonlight, and went back to her work.

Tonight, there was no moon.

When she tapped all the papers into a neat stack and slid them into their folder, a soft hissing cheer, like wind rippling through hundreds of pages, filtered through the lobby. She didn't notice, her mind occupied with a shopping list for the way home, and gratitude that the grocery store was open 24/7. The sound grew louder when she slid her purse out of the bottom drawer of her desk and stood, but the thunder of rain against the front windows muted it. She slid her chair under the desk and turned to make one last round of the library, to make sure no bookworms and bibliophiles had been caught inside, rendered deaf by the intensity of their concentration on a story, or had the volume up too high in their headphones, listening to an audiobook or watching a movie on a tablet. There was always a chance of someone having fallen asleep in one of the meeting rooms.

Or, yes, someone with nasty mischief on their mind, lying in wait until they were alone to steal books or perpetrate some vandalism. Why someone felt it necessary to steal books from the library, when the books were available for anyone to borrow, she found it hard to understand. Most of the time. Sometimes, she had to admit, there was a particular book that was so good, or touched a tender spot in heart and mind, the library patron didn't want to return it.

Or, increasingly, there were others who disapproved of the contents of various books, and stole or defaced them, to keep others from being exposed. When would people learn that the best way to reduce the impact of a book or movie or song was to simply ignore it, shrug it off, give it no attention? Vilifying or mocking a person or thought or piece of art only served to keep it in the public eye and even make it popular.

Her final walk-through complete, and no sign of any loiterers in the shadows, the last librarian headed out through the staff room. She shuddered a little as she put on her coat and tugged it up over her head for partial cover, then pushed the security door open and stepped out. One tug on the handle when the door clicked shut, to assure herself the door was locked, then she was racing across the parking lot to her car.

The humming in the lobby turned to a subtle rattling as the old books in the glass display case jiggled against each other. Trying for some elbow room, if any of them had had any elbows. Shadows seeped through the walls, misty dust reaching from miles away, undeterred and unaffected by the downpour outside. They slipped through the hair-thin gap between the doors, between doors and threshold, through air vents. Through the brick walls of the library. The headlights of the last librarian's car swept across the front of the library and diluted the shadows. Everything went still until the taillights faded away, heading up the long driveway to Butternut Ridge.

"Awake!" an elderly, Scottish-accented voice called, sounding as if it came from miles away.

In actuality, it came from the third shelf on the far right in the display case. The life and the mind that had created the book came from far over the ocean, and that influenced the sound.

The shadows thickened, taking on color and dimension. Even the most avid bibliophile might have shivered to realize those shadows were the ghosts of books, floating in the air, dancing around each other in the lobby, fading in and out, with faint whiffs of dusty paper and moldy leather, old ink, and wood rot in soft puffs, as if on their breath. As if they were living things.

In truth, the books were alive in varying degrees, given life by the minds that formed them and wove their words together. The shadows were the fellows and former traveling partners of the books now caged in the glass case. All across North Olmsted and portions of Northeast Ohio, the books' spirits roused from wherever they now lay, summoned by the longing and loneliness of the old, caged books. Some shadows were thinner and paler than others. They were the true ghosts in the collection, having been destroyed years ago and never returned to the traveling lending library. They had been lost in floods, dropped in snowbanks, torn apart by pets or angry playmates or jealous schoolmates. Their pages had been ripped or soaked, allowed to return to the wood pulp and rags that had formed them. Even tossed into fires, by those with guilty consciences who were ashamed to admit they had been careless and had forgotten to return the books. They didn't want the evidence around to testify against them, to be scolded by librarians they admired, or forced to pay fines by the ones they disliked.

Nearly 200 years ago, the books had been sent from Connecticut, 500 in all, to create a library. The trail had been long and rough and muddy, and some had been damaged, but none of them had been lost. Until the depredations of borrowing and forgetting and time. The shadows of the lost and forgotten books came to reunite with their caged fellows, to share their stored knowledge and stories, and remember, and live again for a little while.

All books long to be read, to share the thoughts and feelings and dreams of their creators. To come alive in the process of transferring images from the past to the present, and hopefully the future. The caged books found little comfort in being admired and wondered at, to have people stand and stare at them and try to make out the titles on their faded and stained and threadbare spines. What use was a book behind a glass wall? It couldn't be read, it couldn't live in the imagination. While they would last another hundred years, cared for and protected, they wouldn't breathe, they wouldn't move. They envied the books that came to visit them, shadows of their former glory, because while they were out there in the wild, those books had a chance of being read. Even the ripped and stained and waterlogged books, with pages and covers missing and spotted with mold and runny ink.

The shadow books whispered to the books in their glass case. Those that had been read or opened or taken to a used bookstore or a repair shop or thrift store told stories of the people who had touched them, the places they had seen, the sounds and smells and images and thoughts they had gathered up in their pages and spines.

Too soon, they ran out of stories. In truth, there were fewer of them every time the longing and hunger to be read and be useful grew strong enough to bring them together.

Tonight, however, was one of those special nights when the magic was stronger. Tonight was the birthday of a creator. The books came together to celebrate and honor one of those who gave them life, and in sharing his words and thoughts, they lived a little more.

At last the whispers, the whiffs of smells from distant places, the echoes of voices and machines and animals all faded away. The silence turned expectant.

"Are we all here?" the Scottish voice asked.

On the third shelf on the far right side, a dark green volume with proud golden letters vibrated a little, moving upright so it no longer leaned against the grayish volume of fifty-eight sermons. The two were good friends, whispering together in the quiet of the library nights when there wasn't enough magic for visitations. Now, the old Scottish book moved away just enough that it didn't lean against the glass on the right or the sermons on the left. It spread its cover and flexed its spine. In the moonlight and magic light, the words on its spine grew brighter.

The Waverly Novels
Rob Roy
Midlothian
Bride of Lammermoor
Legend of Montrose
Ivanhoe

Tonight was a special night. August 15. The birthday of Sir Walter Scott.

"What shall it be?" the old green book asked.

In the many years since they had begun the nighttime reunions, the books had read their contents to each other multiple times. Being books, they never forgot anything. Except, of course, where their pages had been ripped out or the ink had been washed away by water. Still, being books, they loved stories, they loved learning, and they treated the well-known with as much delight as the new.

"*Ivanhoe*, please?" one of the more transparent shadows whispered, pressed against the glass next to the Waverly volume.

Many other books called out with pleasure, seconding the choice.

CHAPTER I

Thus communed these; while to their lowly dome,
The full-fed swine return'd with evening home;
Compell'd, reluctant, to the several sties,
With din obstreperous, and ungrateful cries.

Pope's Odyssey

In that pleasant district of merry England which is watered by the river Don, there extended in ancient times a large forest, covering the greater part of the beautiful hills and valleys which lie between Sheffield and the pleasant town of Doncaster. The remains of this extensive wood are still to be seen at the noble seats of Wentworth, of Warncliffe Park, and around Rotherham. Here haunted of yore the fabulous Dragon of Wantley; here were fought many of the most desperate battles during the Civil Wars of the Roses; and here also flourished in ancient times those bands of gallant outlaws, whose deeds have been rendered so popular in English song.

Such being our chief scene, the date of our story refers to a period towards the end of the reign of Richard I., when his return from his long captivity had become an event rather wished than hoped for by his despairing subjects, who were in the meantime subjected to every species of subordinate oppression. The nobles, whose power had become exorbitant during the reign of Stephen, and whom the prudence of Henry the Second had scarce reduced to some degree of subjection to the crown, had now resumed their ancient license in its utmost extent; despising the feeble interference of the English Council of State, fortifying their castles, increasing the number of their dependants, reducing all around them to a state of vassalage, and striving by every means in their power, to place themselves each at the head of such forces as might enable him to make a figure in the national convulsions which appeared to be impending.

The listening books sighed. The shadowy books clustered together, floating in the lobby, pressed up against the glass to hear better, never feeling the dust motes floating through them.

As long as someone read them and shared their words, books lived.

END

The Oxcart Library

*The Oxcart Library is a collection of books housed, since 1927, at the North Olmsted branch of the Cuyahoga County Library. Consisting of 166 volumes, mostly on subjects relating to theology, travel and farming, it includes the remnant of a 500 volume collection, each volume carefully wrapped in oilcloth, that, in 1829, had been transported 600 miles from New Haven, Connecticut to **Olmsted Township** in a cart pulled by a team of oxen. The original collection was given to the township by Yale University Professor Charles Hyde Olmsted on the condition that it* *change its name from Lenox Twp., which it had been named in 1823, to Olmsted Twp. in honor of his late father, Captain Aaron Olmsted (1753-1806). Captain Olmsted, whose last name has sometimes erroneously been spelled "Olmstead," was one of the original investors in the Connecticut Land Co., formed in 1795. He had secured an option to purchase over 14,000 acres of land in the township originally known simply as "Township 6, Range 15," but had died before he could complete the purchase, his option passing to his heirs.*

The Oxcart Library is considered to be, according to several sources, the first circulating public library in the Western Reserve. According to local North Olmsted historian Luther Paddock, who conducted research for the city's sesquicentennial celebration in 1965, the library was at first "boarded" in houses in the township, with books being lent out to residents from time to time on an informal basis. In 1847, Olmsted Township's board of trustees organized the Olmsted Library Co., which then more formally managed the collection for the next two decades. Annually, the board appointed resident librarians who maintained the books in their homes and kept written records of what was borrowed and returned. Over the years, the collection became reduced in size, in large part as the result of patrons neglecting to return books. In 1868, the Olmsted Library Co. ceased its operations, because the remaining books in its possession were, in the words of the trustees, "useless." The last resident librarian appointed was John D. Taylor.

In 1876, Ellen Bramley, who had purchased John D. Taylor's house, which was located on the corner of Dover Center and Butternut Ridge Rds. in what is today the city of North Olmsted, found 49 books in the attic and returned them to Taylor, who in turn gave them to Arthur A. Stearns, a grandson of David Johnson Stearns, considered to be North Olmsted's first settler and one of the original Olmsted Twp. Trustees. Stearns, an attorney who later became President of the Board of Trustees of Cleveland Public Library, kept the books for decades in the attic of his house. In 1927, while he was serving as Vice-President of the Board, Stearns donated these books, and several more from the original collection which had been recently found, to the Cleveland Public Library, which arranged for them to be sent to the new North Olmsted branch of the Library's County Department (today, the Cuyahoga County Public Library). Over the years, additional volumes from the original collection have been recovered and "returned" to the "Oxcart Library," as the collection became known in circa 1950. Of particular note, in 1961, North Olmsted Librarian Ruth Helt reached out publicly to the North Olmsted community to look for and return books from the original collection. As a result of her efforts, a large number of books, which had been lying in attics, old barns, and elsewhere in North Olmsted, were found and returned, increasing the number of volumes in the Oxcart Library to its present size.

James Dubelko
From https://case.edu/ech/articles/o/oxcart-library

On the road to publication, Michelle fell into fandom in college and has 40+ stories in various SF and fantasy universes. She has a bunch of useless degrees in theater, English, film/communication, and writing. Even worse, she has over 100 books and novellas with multiple small presses, in science fiction and fantasy, YA, suspense, women's fiction, and sub-genres of romance.

Her official launch into publishing came with winning first place in the Writers of the Future contest in 1990. She was a finalist in the EPIC Awards competition multiple times, winning with Lorien in 2006 and The Meruk Episodes, I-V, in 2010, and was a finalist in the Realm Awards competition, in conjunction with the Realm Makers convention.

Her training includes the Institute for Children's Literature; proofreading at an advertising agency; and working at a community newspaper. She is a tea snob and freelance edits for a living (MichelleLevigne@gmail.com for info/rates), but only enough to give her time to write. Her newest crime against the literary world is to be co-managing editor at Mt. Zion Ridge Press and launching the publishing co-op, Ye Olde Dragon Books. Be afraid … be very afraid.

www.Mlevigne.com
www.MichelleLevigne.blogspot.com
www.YeOldeDragonBooks.com
www.MtZionRidgePress.com
@MichelleLevigne